PRAISE FOR
HOME MAKING

"An intricate exploration of family and home, of mother and child, of friends, of women, and written with both precision and style."

—Weike Wang, author of *Chemistry*

"In this remarkable novel, Lee Matalone fashions a world of rich and nuanced characters. Matalone has created something original, almost kaleidoscopic, as she constructs the interwoven tales of the characters who each strive to form a home. She writes skillfully about relationships, living and dying, and love. Cleverly and beautifully rendered, this is the work of an author plunging beneath the surface, into the very heart of what fabricates our inner and outer lives. This is a smart, uncanny, and ambitious debut."

—Nina McConigley, author of *Cowboys and East Indians*, winner of the PEN Open Book Award

"*Home Making* is subtle, funny, and original. An enormously moving novel about learning to make a home and, ultimately, a life."

—Erin Somers, author of *Stay Up with Hugo Best*

"In *Home Making*, Lee Matalone has written the debut novel of the year. Structurally bold and metaphorically rich, Matalone constructs a whole new world from the empty spaces inside us all. In *Home Making*, Matalone provides a rich, new blueprint of how we find meaning in the places we inhabit, the people we know, and ultimately how we continue to build that home, which is our self. Brilliant."

—Scott McClanahan, author of *The Sarah Book*

Home Making

Home
Making

A NOVEL

Lee Matalone

HARPER  PERENNIAL

NEW YORK • LONDON • TORONTO • SYDNEY • NEW DELHI • AUCKLAND

HARPER ● PERENNIAL

HarperCollins books may be purchased for educational, business, or sales promotional use. For information, please email the Special Markets Department at SPsales@harpercollins.com.

FIRST EDITION

Designed by Jen Overstreet

Library of Congress Cataloging-in-Publication Data has been applied for.

ISBN 978-0-06-295366-7 (pbk.)

20 21 22 23 24   LSC   10 9 8 7 6 5 4 3 2 1

To my mother

Question your teaspoons.
—Georges Perec

Home Making

War Child

Before, before—a young woman, in a modest but pristine apartment in Tokyo, paints a castle on paper, unlike any castle in Japan. *Where is this castle?* her mother, who secretly writes poetry on gum wrappers, whose ancestors created beauty with katana rather than pen, asks her daughter. She starts to answer, but her mother grabs the paper and flips it over. *Your mind is a ship*, she says. *It will take you away from me and leave me here alone. Your hair is dirty. Why don't you do something about that?* So this young woman, her name lost to the wrinkles of history, washes her hair, and it is clean and black and straight and falls at the arch of her bony shoulders. She is all bones, lanky and bendy like a strip of Wrigley's. *We need . . .* her mother says, and she probably said more tea or meriken-ko or toothpaste, and sent her daughter out into the noontime street, into the crowded Tokyo Saturday, where families are sitting in parks or visiting grave sites of

their mothers and fathers and grandmothers, who were un-
lucky enough to live in Hiroshima or Nagasaki. Though the
events happened six years ago, these relatives still come here
in order to remember, to show that they have not moved on
entirely to rockabilly and *Look* and Hirohito's beloved *Super-
man*, that they can still lay white chrysanthemums on their
ancestors' tombs and thank their new god they never had to
see Uncle Ryu like that, like they say he was found, and she is
walking right beside the monument and she stops.

A man in uniform with white skin and blue eyes is kneel-
ing in front of one of these tombs, and she may or may not
have been angry at this intruder, at his intrusion, but more
likely what she is feeling is her heart coming alive in her cotton shirt because he is different and beautiful but likely just
different, beauty often being simply an aberration from the
norm, a departure from her mother, from her own black hair,
and because she is just as bold as her daughter will be, she
will go up to this man and tap him on the shoulder and ask
him if he would like to take a walk with her to Kinokuniya,
where she is on the way to buy flour and toothpaste, where
they also sell frozen Salisbury steak paired with carrots and
peas, and his face is long and bony, and she identifies with
this, and they walk off together down the cobblestone street.

Things happen, including a conversation in a park (she
speaks un peu Français) and a sneaking out to go to a club
where other white men dance with brown girls, and they
drink French aperitifs and Japanese whiskey and are drunk
but not too drunk to recognize joy, and they go to his room
and she leaves a kiss on his cheek in the dark of the morning—

she has slept too long, but she knows her mother won't wake for another three hours, and she is running down the street, back to the apartment, and inside, now, a problem is growing.

That problem is Ayumi.

Ayumi never knows her name is Ayumi because her mother, upon finding out she is pregnant, leaves home, prostrates herself at the door of a hospital, crying out in the midst of labor pains, and signs the baby over to the state. Which the state doesn't want, because this baby is a baby with blue eyes and brown skin, and, to make matters worse, this baby is female. No one will want this baby. Some Franciscan nuns, some sisters, take this baby and place it in their orphanage, their brown faces peeking out from behind white habits, brown fingers reaching out of draping white sleeves to push the brown children with blue and green eyes on a merry-go-round painted with faded yellow ducks, and, months later, an American officer comes in with his wife and this child overhears one of the sisters say *Loveland*, the name like a line of poetry, the child who has poetry in her blood, and this toddler, right as the American officer is walking by, reaches out a tiny, two-year-old hand and touches the arm of his jacket, and he stops walking—he had his eyes on a baby boy on the other side of the room, a strong-haunched Japanese boy—but he stops and he swivels and he looks at her, this child with blue eyes and brown skin, a girl, but that doesn't matter, this child is his.

Back to America, back to the States with his big-boned, not-so-beautiful blond wife and his three blond-haired, blue-eyed, white-skinned natural-borns, of six and eight and ten years old, in a plane back over the Pacific, over California, the McDonald's arches glowing in the sun, which this grown Hāfu will remember seeing from the plane, though her own daughter will disavow this, will say that there is no way *anyone* could possibly see the Golden Arches from up in a plane, much less a two-year-old, and they speed over the Mojave, with its yipping coyotes and endless dust, and they land in another desert, in Tucson, a place without castles but with chrysanthemums on graves, just for different, less atomic reasons.

And let's say that she is the only brown-skinned girl in any bassinet in that residential development in 1953, anno domini, the only brown-skinned, blue-eyed girl riding her bicycle down War Bonnet Lane, hair pigtailed in the way that makes everyone think she is Navajo. Whatever she is, they know she isn't *white*, which means that she doesn't fit into this world of McDonald's arches and *Cosmopolitan*, though by her twelfth birthday the neighborhood recognizes that she is undeniably beautiful, a petite girl (yet, like her Wrigley-boned birth mother, all legs) with petite freckles, a petite nose, and a petite frame forged in bronze—*bronze*, a shade that has become culturally desirable, as long as the shade isn't *black*, more alluring than the pasty skin of her adopted mother, her varicose veins hidden under tan nylons. She will learn that her beauty is a problem, that this is not something her mother can suffer, and her father will be oblivious—he now promoted to brigadier general, always off in a hushed room with a group of men in pressed suits, and her bigger brothers will protect her from these abuses, sometimes, and she sews the holes in their jeans for them, because she loves them and they are not a wealthy family, military, unlike but also like her family in Japan, who she will never know, they aren't really her family either.

Cybil and boys. She discovers boys, rides on the backs of their motorcycles, sneaks out and eats mole in Mexican dives on the South Side, and people still think she is Navajo but they don't care, because she is *foxy*, and perhaps more importantly she has something to say. She devours Friedan and Rhys and Plath, and boys, at least, at first, cannot help but fall at her feet, especially in those bell-bottoms. And she gets out of the desert, because she has known since she was a Navajo on a trike that she wanted to be a doctor, which is what she does. She leaves the desert to get her bachelor's at a liberal arts college in the icy Midwest, where, in the winter, the boys (*always* the boys) have garbage can races in the frozen parking lot, and she likes one or two of these boys, but she is very focused on her studies—not too focused, because she is smart, MENSA smart, and she doesn't have to do much studying, just a little more than her roommate, who has a photographic memory, which she will always envy, as she will repeatedly tell her own daughter.

And she meets a man there, a handsome man, one kind of like her father, a man with a heroic inclination, and he can speak of subatomic particles and Gertrude Stein in the same breath, and this she finds irresistible, because she loves words but she also wants to deliver babies, and so she falls for this man, Neil, a type of man whose complexity she will warn her daughter about, even though he doesn't go to her school and lives in Chicago, but he drives to her every other weekend, and in the summer they go to Yellowstone, where they take thirty-mile day hikes and camp out in the backwoods, always with a bear bell on her hip, and he takes photographs (of waterfalls, her breasts) and she draws pictures of the local flora, wildflowers mostly—her mother, too, could draw—and so they spend these undergraduate years like this, and when she receives the acceptance letter in the mail to a medical school back in the desert and one in Chicago that is private and celebrated but also much more expensive, she decides to return home, and he decides to return home with her.

This is when she first realizes that she cannot rely on men. This is still when her baby is not yet a glimmer in her eye, when she's still focused on her studies, when the smell of McDonald's PlayPlaces make her nauseous, the sight of a child not instigating any biological response, and she is busy, busy, busy, mastering the body, attending lectures, dissecting cadavers, drawing blood, washing her hands, starting IVs, slicing into the abdomens of women she's never spoken to, washing her hands, placing her hands into someone's womb, not sleeping, not seeing Neil, learning the names of medicines, the words swirling in her dreams, giving epidurals, not sleeping, not seeing Neil, washing her hands. And when she comes home one day, she realizes he is not there, that he has not been there for a while.

(What happened to Neil is what happens to all former loves: He left her but he never really left her.)

The first man, but not the last to go. The second is to be the father of her child, a charmer, not a Renaissance man like the first one, but one she believes has good intentions, and their courtship is short and it is easy, and they both agree that they want to get out of this desert, to a place with trees that shed leaves and snowfall and good schools, because now she wants a baby. She loves the smell of babies, all babies, of their baby shampoo, their wisps of hair she likes to wind around her fingers in the aisles of supermarkets. This is the sign that she's ready, and so they move across the country, to a place of soft hills, to Virginia, into a house with a green yard and big windows through which she can already see a child rolling, laughing in the green, and she's a doctor now, and in this new place she starts her own practice, and she's establishing herself, and she is ready to have this baby.

And *boy* does this baby come, and the labor is nothing like she could have imagined, though she has helped hundreds of women go through this same process, and she knows the scientific names for everything, but nothing can prepare her for the moments of pushing and breathing and panting and crying and the feeling of her uterine walls contracting and the moment when she hears that first cry of the baby, her baby, as she enters the world, a fucked-up world, one with bad men and bad women and cruel fathers and cruel mothers, but nothing compares to this feeling of this baby, her baby, and this child falls into another doctor's hands, and this mother is exhausted and overjoyed and all she can do is give the doctor a thumbs-up, and she lets her head fall back against the soaked paper pillow.

And then the baby is placed in her arms, and it's like the light of the room dims except for a halo around her and this baby. And whatever the men do—they come and go, lovers, boyfriends come and go—she will have this moment, and this life with this baby. And she will not be a perfect mother. She will give her daughter her eccentricities, a daughter who will feel that her mother is cold and removed sometimes. She is no Hallmark card of Motherhood. But this mother will do anything for her child, because she has a responsibility to show her the goodness in a world full of despair, to show her that she is loved when many babies out there are not loved, are given away, left in orphanages, in the hopes that some man and some woman, or some man and man or woman and woman, will walk by the right crib at the very moment that the baby extends a hand and grabs their coat.

This baby, Chloe, will not suffer that. She will be loved, from hospital bed to home.

Chloe

I want to build a home. Or, rather, I want to take this existing house and turn it into something where happiness can bloom. I will start with one room, stripping the yellowed wallpaper, melting and scrubbing old glue in yellow gloves. Or do I start with the floors? Do I have to refinish the floors first, so that the shavings don't scratch up the fresh paint? Maybe I have that backward. Maybe I should paint first, and then do the floors, so that the paint doesn't drip onto the newly refinished wood.

I built a home once, not so long ago, but I have forgotten the how-tos. How to re-grout shower tile. How to hang a picture on a stud. As if my brain has decided that recollecting was detrimental to my survival.

Someone built this house for a family. I constantly feel like I'm intruding on someone else's domestic life. Every time I forget to turn off the faucet when I'm boiling water, I think that a mother will run over and chastise me. When I play music late at night, I feel like a little boy will come down the stairs, onesied-feet padding on the hardwood, and say "I'm trying to sleep. Will you please turn that down?"

This doesn't feel like my home, I tell people. Part of me knows that this wasn't built for me.

This house's architecture isn't specific to one region. It doesn't have terracotta tiles for its roof or adobe bricks for its form like those in Tucson or Santa Fe. It isn't a shotgun house that runs long and narrow, the humidity seeping through the un-insulated walls, as they do deep in the American South. It's a sturdy Foursquare, as Americana as you can get, older, but the bones are good. The structure of this house is sound.

The neighborhood, too, is just right. Set on the outskirts of a small city, the nearest neighbor more than spitting distance, my house sits on two and a half acres in view of the rolling Blue Ridge Mountains. Large hills, really, but I don't need more than that.

In fact, when I would hear the word "house," this is what I would think of. This is the Platonic form of a house. It's everything I ever wanted.

There are more rooms in this house than I know what to do with. I am responsible for a kitchen and a pantry and a mudroom and a garage and a living room and a dining room and a guest room and a guest bathroom and a master bedroom and a master bathroom and even an attic that I can access by pulling on a tattered red string.

I have only been in the attic once, when the Realtor first showed me the house. I asked her to take me up there, so she pulled the red string and we walked up the creaky wooden stairs and ascended into a dark, dusty, empty space. No old trunks or rocking chairs left behind by the former owners. Just vacancy.

But I have not been up there since. What would I do if I stepped on a rusty nail and couldn't get back down? Would anyone find me up there?

Living alone requires an extra level of pragmatism. Lock the doors. Check the carbon monoxide detector's batteries. Read the labels on the pills before swallowing them in the haze of two in the morning, as there will be no one to find you.

Peanut butter. Coffee. Bread. Toilet paper. I text Beau with a list. He is running my errands, performing the tasks of domesticity I am not yet ready to perform on my own.

The peanut butter isn't even for you, is it? he texts back. It's for Tito, isn't it?

The truth is this: I am not worried about all of the space, so much space with not even a coffee table or couch or bed frame. This place does not feel empty.

Beau, a sculptor of the delicate, of cotton and hair and tulle and leaves, often reassures me, *As the great sculptor of pirouetting steel, Richard Serra, said, space is material.*

Perhaps all the possibility would make some people anxious. I know my mother and Beau worry about me feeling lonely in this house, about my being alone. They look at me with those eyes that squint and narrow, as if those eyes could hug me in close and make me feel like I'm not surrounded by so much space, that I'm not so alone.

But I'm fine here. That may be hard to believe, but I'm excited by this empty house, by the kitchen that needs renovating, the master bath that needs updating, by the possibilities.

Would anyone worry about a man moving into a house alone? How about two adult women, unmatched romantically? No. Of course they wouldn't. Only a woman alone in a house with a dog, me, in other words, would make someone worry. A woman with a cat even fits into some prefabricated notion, the safety of a stereotype, an innocuous pink rubber mold. But with a dog, with Tito, no. No one takes comfort in a single woman with only a dog for a companion.

Beau's caring manifests in a number of ways. On my porch and in my inbox, I find everything from philosophy tomes to DIY home renovation blogs to architectural manifestos. He crosses out the titles in Sharpie, adds his own. *One Perspective* and *Some Kind of Inspiration* and *See?*

It took ten years for Herman Wallace to decide what he wanted his home to look like. After thirty years in solitary confinement (for a murder he did not commit), Wallace received a letter from an art student at a West Coast collegiate temple. She wanted to know, "What kind of house do you, a man who lives in a six-foot-by-nine-foot cell, dream of?"

While living in a cell at Angola, that notorious modern plantation, he dreamt of tulips, Adirondacks perched on a second-floor balcony, portraits of Tubman, Turner, Brown, a bathtub as big as his cell of confinement, windows, windows,

windows. For ten years, he contemplated what his concept of home looked like.

"In front of the house," he wrote to her, "I have three squares of gardens. The gardens are the easiest to imagine. I would like for guests to smile and walk through flowers all year long."

This is my duty: to realize the fullness of this task.

"I'm going to send you some vitamins," my mother says. She is a voice coming out of a speaker on the kitchen island. My hands are not busy but I've taken to using the speaker for all calls. The calm that comes from the way the house fills up with sound.

"I appreciate that, Mom, but I can get my own."

"But you won't. We both know you won't do that right now." In staccato form, she reprimands her mutt, not *Ti-to, Ti-to!* but *Hen-ri! Hen-ri!* "Are you sure you don't want me to come and see you?"

"I'm so busy right now. I wouldn't know what to do with you. Soon though."

"You know you don't have to entertain me. I can sit. I can read. I can even help do whatever you need help doing." From the island, a cacophony of barking. From the floor, Tito tilts his head at me wondering, *Will we have a visitor, finally?*

"Soon, Mom." *Soon, Tito.*

"I'll send vitamins," she says.

I should be landscaping, caulking, painting, unpacking, organizing, but instead I'm going through my social media pages, looking for ghosts to haunt. There is a high school sweetheart who nearly burnt down his college apartment trying to make MDMA, a fling who I accompanied to his AA meetings. There is M., but there has always been M., a figure of longing who came into my life before Pat, when we were both students, he a graduate student and I an undergraduate. If never sated, some affections can live on for years, dormant yet capable of being awoken at the stroke of a key, the dispatch of a text message.

Mostly though, I harass telemarketers.

"I thought cell phones were a safe space," I say. "But I suppose it was inevitable that you'd find a way."

"Well, no one has landlines nowadays," the man selling home and garden magazines says. "We have to connect with you somehow."

"You know, I appreciate you connecting."

"We don't hear that a lot. So thank you."

"I just mean, you seem like a nice person, despite your job's tendency to irritate."

"I appreciate that, too. Could I interest you in a subscription to *Good Housekeeping*?"

"Do you have anything else?"

"*House Beautiful. Country Living. Woman's Day.*"

"What about *Garden & Gun*?"

"*Garden & Gun* is not a part of the Hearst Group."

"Too bad."

"Perhaps you'd rather something for your husband? *Esquire* makes for a nice gift. Or is he more of the *Car and Driver* type?"

"Good luck out there. I have to go."

"Tell me what you need. We can help."

"Good luck, I said."

"Well, you too."

From last week's doorstep book from Beau: "It can be hard to walk into a freshly decorated house without feeling preemptively sad at the decay impatiently waiting to begin: how soon the walls will crack, the white cupboards will yellow, and the carpets stain."

After all my hard work, after all the walls are painted and the windows caulked and the tulips cut and placed in the kitchen table's vase, time starts back at the house almost immediately. There's a certain undeniable futility to this work of home building.

HOUSE TO-DO: TO BEGIN

- Buy paint for guest bathroom (*Honeymilk* or *Lily of the Valley*?).
- Build raised garden beds—> Call Beau.
- Dust everything, again.
- Wash pillows. Buy pillow protectors. It may be too late for these pillows. Maybe order new pillows.
- Call exterminator. Sounds at night, scratching. Raccoons in walls, in attic? Bats on the beams?
- Consideration: Is a yoga room cheesy/over the top? Would an altar be gauche? Incense and candles and a gong? No gong. But maybe one of those little waterfall machines that you plug into the wall to create a tranquil white noise. Tell no one about this room.

* * *

Objects contain parts of the people who own them. Though my mother's adoptive mother died before I had a chance to know her, her emerald earrings still gleam with a hint of her cruelty. With Pat, what is left of our philosophical disagreements is contained in a coffee table book of dilapidated barns and wooden houses taken over by grasses and wildflowers.

"That's something I can't settle with," Pat, my sick husband, once said. "The fact that people are obsessed with decaying buildings and dying cities."

"You can't deny that an old barn is beautiful," I said.

"But the fact that people find it beautiful says something. People find beauty in loss. At what point does that quest for death become a self-fulfilling prophecy?"

When people go, the things they leave behind can feel haunted. A father can take your left ventricle and a husband can take your frontal lobe, leaving behind a tea kettle, a lamp shade from Bed Bath & Beyond. A wooden spoon can hold the existential weight of a family Bible while you turn into a shell.

Once, my mother told me about visiting Bergen-Belsen as a child, ten years after the camps had been liberated. Even then, she said, you could smell the smoke.

It is very possible that it can be too late for happiness.

Le Corbusier believed that the function of a house was simple, to provide 1. *A shelter against heat, cold, rain, thieves, and the inquisitive. 2. A receptacle for light and sun. 3. A certain number of cells appropriated to cooking, work, and personal life.*

I do not want to live in a cell. I want rooms and warmth and inquisitive minds. I refuse to live in a receptacle.

Tɪᴛᴏ: To-Do
- Bathe Tito (hypoallergenic shampoo).
- Take to vet for annual vaccinations–> Ask if he needs kennel cough if he's never at the dog park/around other dogs.
- Buy the good wet food, just this once. These are special circumstances.
- Look into getting companion. Dogs get lonely.
   - Two dogs = easier than one. For me and him. Mutual entertainment/engagement.
      - Large dog or another little dog? Large dog: Would s/he fit in my car? Would possibly need a differ- ent, roomier car.
         - New (used) car: hatchback or sedan? Or maybe a pick-up would be more practical. I could use it for the garden, for moving dirt or paint cans or wood. In case I need to do any repairs to the shed, I may need to transport wood.
            - How many miles do I have on my car right now? Check into this. Pushing 120, I think. Really time to get a new car, one big enough for two dogs, regardless of size. Not good for children either. I may want a Pyr- enees. I will need a car I don't care about littering with tufts of thick white hair. A truck, a big red truck with an extended cab

for the dogs, with a metal floor. No carpet,
no frills, for me and Tito and the Pyrenees.
- Brush Tito. Then dust. Dust everything.

I've always fantasized about homes. I've drawn out versions
of my fantasy-dwelling in sketchbooks and on notepads
while sitting on a tattered mid-century couch in a bungalow
I wished were mine. In my early twenties, pre-Pat, I traveled
around the country in search of the perfect town where I could
put down roots. Renting in some town in some other person's
house, I would have fantasies of ripping out the kitchen cabinets and placing open shelves where I could display my cook-
books and stack my white plates, where I could set a planter
containing a single stem of purple orchids.

In the *Times*, there is an article about people who get very
attached to houses, as if loving a house were a peculiar thing.
I click on the headline, but I do not read a word.

I thought our home was a castle. I thought those walls
could keep us safe.

More from Le Corbusier, someone I think may very well have
been a madman: "Home life today is being paralysed by the
deplorable notion that we must have furniture."

But then again, it is easy to forget that a chair, a table, is
a refinement, not a utility. Think of the Japanese eating on
pads on the floor. They have thrived without the presence of
a boudeuse or buffet in their homes.

I should be honest with myself: I will have to stick a Womb

Chair in the corner, a reproduction, anyway, something to embrace me.

> *home base*
> *home life*
> *hometown*
> *home grown*
> *home body*
> *home sick*
> *home away from home*
> *no place like home*
> *E.T. phone home*
> *run away from home*

Can you be too old to run away from home? Can a full-grown woman run away from home? Can she run away from a home that was forced upon her? She should be allowed to, if that's what she wants.

Just as President Kubitschek constructed Brasília in the hopes that its Niemeyers would usher in an age of Modern values, I can build this house in the shapes that will foster my own ideals. Niemeyer thought that the aerospacial curves of his buildings could bring progress to Brazil's forests. The stark white concrete pillars could teach reason and order to the people of undeveloped Brazil (an interesting, if not disturbing idea, colonizing the mind through architecture).

I can set the kitchen table for four. I can make sure the bed in the guest room is always made.

nova mulher, Americana e moderna

That's all you need? Beau texts back.

   I copy and paste. Peanut butter. Coffee. Bread. Toilet paper.
That can't be all you need, he texts. Tell me what you need.

I have been alone in this house for a month thinking about what color to paint the hall bathroom.

Consider it building a watchtower, I tell people when they ask why I bought a house so close to where Pat and I once shared a home. If he will not let me be with him while he dies, then I can make sure that nothing or no one else can hurt him. From here, I can still feel like I am doing my duty, like I am being the wife.

Mom and Beau keep telling me not to rush things. One room at a time, they tell me.

   But I'm not trying to build an entire city, I tell them. I'm just trying to rearrange these pieces of my life and turn them into something that resembles a home.

   One room, they reiterate. Start with the space with the smallest square footage and work up from there. Think of Rome, they say.

I am unblackening my teeth, a white strip adhered to my smile. Beau stands in the doorframe of the bathroom, flipping through a celebrity rag, while I hover over the sink, the blue cardboard box with its disembodied mouth glaring up at me from the basin. Beau says that my teeth are big and beautiful and that when I feel like smiling again my smile should glisten. He does not say, *smile*, as some men do. He just says, when you *feel like* smiling again, *you should glow, baby.* He says, in that edifying way of his, that Japanese women, upon marriage, once painted their teeth black, a sign of their commitment. I say, actually, I told you that, Beau. *Nice try.*

But I am no longer a wife, not quite anymore. I must paint my teeth white, though I still feel the black paint opaquing my incisors. I must go back to when they grew in ivory. I must go back to the beginning.

Ayumi

Haha Haha Haha. We are all crying this word though we do not know what it means. Some of the older boys and girls say it to us little ones. They run up to the windows, make binoculars of their eyes and say, *Haha is coming. We are all getting Hahas. Haha Haha Haha.* I like the sound of the word. My eighteen-month-old lips love this word. I push the "H" out of my mouth like I'm trying to make a halo of fog on the window that passes light above my crib.

When we *Haha*-ed, the sisters would smile, pinch our cheeks, kiss our ears. They thought we were laughing. Or, they wanted to believe we were laughing. What those sisters went through, seeing babies dropped off day by day by day, blue eyes and mud hair, green eyes and soybean skin, soon to be motherless, fatherless, haha-less, chichi-less. They must have had so much sadness. They must have felt so guilty at what adults like them were incapable of.

Sunflowers. Sister Mayu wears sunflower-yellow socks that pop out of her white habit and a headscarf like a bridal veil. One of the older girls asks, "Mayu, when are you getting married? May I come to your wedding? Will you have a daughter? Can you name her after me? I'm your sweetness, Mayu. I'm so sah-weeeet."

When the soldiers in the cardboard-starch suits visit, they always offer the bigger children candy. Hershey's and Wrigley's, things we children have never seen. Keiko, one of the other children, comes over to the edge of my crib, smacking her pretty pink mouth, her hair stringy and blond and bobbed and her eyes black gobstoppers. *Want one, Ayumi? You can't have one! Too young! Too young! One day though. I'll share my candy with you. One day, when you're my little sister and we go home, I will share my candy with you. But not the chocolate. The chocolate is all mine. Potty time, Ayumi? Do you need to go to the potty? We are all going to the potty.* And she lifts me out of my crib, perching my little rotund body on her little hip, not even a hip, a little ledge of bone and skin. The nuns feed us little ones and feed us and feed us until we are round and happy-looking. The older kids, the ones who can handle themselves, who have begun to understand the choices adults have to make, have to go without, sometimes.

My hair. Thick and black. All of us infants have the same haircut, as if the sisters overturned a rice bowl and shorn helmets around its porcelain rim.

Potty time. A row of porcelain bowls topped with bare butts. What a vision! We alien children perched on bowls, our sweaters hanging over our hibu, dutifully sitting, waiting for others to go, and maybe we go while we're waiting for the other children to go, because we are sitting and we are bored and what else is there to do but kuso.

It is said that children cannot remember anything below the age of three, but I remember lying in that crib, waiting. I remember Sister Mayu's sunflower socks and the boys who picked on the blond girls before the mud-headed girls. I was seeing the white men and women with hair that matched the skin that matched the eyes, bodies coordinated and coherent, seeing these men and women look around the room, scanning the heads and faces in cribs, the rug rats playing with blocks on the floor, the bigger girls and boys working on their lessons, the white men and women scanning for the ones that looked like them, mostly, not the ones that looked like us, the ones that looked like they didn't belong anywhere, the ones whose only home was in this place, a place of funny white hats that looked like veils (but would never be veils) and yellow socks and sterile tile floors. This is what we had to call home, not the world of our hahas outside the window, or the world of our fathers that lay on the other edge of the sea. Here was home. How could we not remember what that was like?

When you're in an orphanage for the first two years of your life, you grow up knowing that motherhood is a choice, not a given state. You don't just get pregnant, suffer the nine months, give birth, and become Mother. You choose this title. At the formative moment when the doctor takes the baby from your body, cuts the cord, checks vitals, you have some options. From that moment, the choices emerge.

Option one: When the doctor puts the baby in your arms, you can cross them, shake your head, say, *Not my baby*, give the baby to the state, allow him to become the child of a devoted Mother, someone who has consciously decided she wants the title.

Option two: When the doctor puts the baby in your arms, you can take the baby, sway the baby, take the baby home, put the baby to sleep, but you don't like the time the baby takes, the time the baby takes away from you, from your independence, your romantic and sexual pleasures, so the baby becomes an afterthought, something that looks cute in pretty pink pants and dresses with a little ribbon snapped to the single wisp of hair but not something worth exchanging your vanity for, and the baby grows up, becomes a toddler, becomes a preteen, becomes a young adult, becomes an adult, knowing that this mother never *really* wanted to be a mother, that this was not the path she wanted, that she never committed to Motherhood.

Option three: You can throw yourself into this endeavor of Motherhood. You can take that baby into your arms, stick her to your breast, give her a home, all that she wants (choices), all that she doesn't want (discipline), and she will grow up knowing that Motherhood is a beautiful thing, a beautiful beautiful beautiful thing.

Is it clear what I chose for Chloe?

For those that didn't have happy childhoods, there are two ways to parent, if you choose to enter into Motherhood: You can hammer into your own child the lessons you were forced to learn, spanking the way you were spanked, refusing to dote the way your parents refused to dote on you, to show the child that the world is cyclical and that you don't deserve anything better than what you yourself got from your own mother and father. Or, you, the parent with the unhappy childhood, can say, *I'm going to give this child everything I didn't have.* You can shower this child with love and affection, plastic toys that break after a few days of soft play or expensive, organic French toys made of wood that cost more than your week's worth of groceries. You decide, *This child will never not feel love, she will never have the opportunity to not feel loved*, and you will commit entirely to this thing, you will give everything to this child, to this role of Mother, even at the expense of your own personal gratification and independence, because what matters is showing your child that not all people are hopeless, that things can be good. They can.

You choose this second option because you understand you can never forget the childhood you were delivered.

On your mother's fiftieth birthday, after months of physical distance, you lean in to hug her, but then the smell of cigarettes in her hair triggers a certain memory you've done all you can to exorcise.

Five years old, crinoline fanned around me. The tree's popcorn illuminated red and green. Under and around the tree waited boxes and bags, all wrapped up by my mother. My father was not around to do the wrapping, but Christmas morning there he was, slippered and robed with a cup of coffee and a knee to share. I wrapped my little hands around his calf and watched

my siblings open their gifts. A three-speed for my brother
Terry; a denim jacket for my eldest, Russ; a robin's-egg-blue
dress hand-sewn by my mother, the fabric picked out by my
sister, Jean, and style modeled after a photo she saw of Grace
Kelly in *Look*. After opening the box, Jean rushed upstairs.
For ten minutes she primped in the long mirror in her bedroom, fantasizing about some boy taking her out for a drive
in the dry desert night. When she came downstairs, she was
all seriousness. Against the hardness of her face, the baby
blue of her dress registered steel.

Your turn, my mother said. Daddy pointed at the box, my
box.

The wrapping paper featured women with platinum and
fire-engine-red coiffures, permed and pressed and dyed to
perfection, their hourglass waists cinched into air. These la-
dies were what my mother and Jean aspired to, the women
they identified as the apotheosis of beauty, faces powdered
and lightened and lightened to resemble marble. Whiteness,
above all else. Then (as now, certainly, too), pigment stood for
something dirtied, something foreign, something certainly
not American. *Jap. Nip. Tojo.*

*From the TV, a gray and white rabbit in a clean white uni-
form says, handing out popsicles prepared maliciously, contents
containing grenades, "Here, one for you, Monkeyface. Here you
are, Slant Eyes!"*

I tore at these women, severing their bodices from their
skirts, guillotining the made-up alabaster faces from swan
necks.

And there, beneath the wrapping paper, a black face. This
baby doll, with a belly bubbling out of a gingham nappy,

arms akimbo in some ambiguous state (Was she reaching out for Mommy or recoiling in fear?). The baby wore black pin-curls shorn tight around her ink-black face. Her eyes and cherry-red lips glinted with shock.

My mother, watching from her own chair, fully made up, dressed in a dress to match my sister's.

You have the same eyes.

We didn't, but we were both shades of brown she registered as Other. We were no Grace, no beauty to cut out of a magazine and paste on the wall.

Jap. Nip. Tojo. Slant Eyes.

What I remember: the cruelty of a cigarette, white against her lips.

When I worked, when I could not leave Chloe alone in her crib in the middle of the night to rush off to help a soon-to-be mother, a could-be mother, another person filled in my gaps. A nanny. An au pair. But we never called her that. We did not use that word. It was understood that she would be a part of our family (au pair = at equal, not a daughter, not a wife, but something else). When Chloe turned three, my husband decided we were not the family he wanted, so what was I to do? Au pair, my answer.

They were Rita and Lisa and Cecilia. From age three to thirteen, Chloe was in their partial care.

Rita: A forty-eight-year-old woman from Jackson, Mississippi, whose life was Chloe. She had grown children who no longer needed her. As a child, her own mother called her *Pig Nose* and cut her hair short under a mixing bowl, locking her in a closet if she resisted. One of her three brothers, a long-haul truck driver, was now in prison for dragging an elderly woman into a field behind a convenience store and raping her with a pipe. She coveted Chloe, guarded her like her own.

Lisa: A twenty-eight-year-old English woman who wore jeans from the men's section of Kohl's. She was fond of taking Chloe to the pool in the summers and driving with her foot hanging out the window. She was a born-again Christian, but I asked her to keep her religious beliefs to herself.

Cecilia: A thirty-three-year-old woman from Accra fond of leggings and *Ellen*. In the era of dial-up Internet, Chloe and her friend, pre-teens, used the basement's phone line to call the upstairs phone line, adopting the voice of Kiefer Sutherland in the movie *Phone Booth*, which was about a sniper targeting a man trapped in a phone booth. As I recall, Cecilia chased Chloe around the house with a wooden spoon. She was concerned about this sniper.

These women did the work I couldn't. They were surrogate face wipers, shoe-tying instructors, snack makers, TV guides, reading tutors, soccer coaches, good-night kisses.

They were many things, all those things, but they were never Mother. That was the title I chose, the life I committed to. That role was mine.

Ten-year-old Chloe wants to run the tap, her girlish foot tapping on the bathroom tile.

"Hot as can be," I say.

The water coming out of the bathtub faucet steams. Her eyes fixate on the steam, as if witnessing a gorge hissing to life, some great environmental occurrence.

"Are you getting in?" she asks.

Yes. I nod. *I will be the first to step on the moon.*

She watches the rolls of my body, how the water fills in around each fold. She will always feel safe in the water.

"Would you bring me the newspaper, please?"

"I'm getting in," she announces but she's already undressing. It is January and her body is white, topped off with an unruly, coffee-colored coiffure. She is not good at brushing her hair, though I'm teaching her, slowly. Stomach. There, her baby fat is shedding, puberty chiseling away belly. Still, no hips. But they're coming. Then we will have things to talk about.

She dips the toes of her right foot first, shrinks back.

"Too hot?" I turn on the cold, just for a minute. "Better? See? Feel?"

She manages to stick one whole skinny leg into the bath, perching like a flamingo. She has been taking ballet classes for six months. We still have sixteen months before she exchanges slippers for softball cleats.

"Get in," I say. "It feels nice."

"What's thirty-four across?" she asks.

"Italian cheese city."

"Parmesan," she says, smirking, a sweet smirk.

Already, she is too much of a smart ass. This will get her in trouble. She will never be satisfied. I'm trying to teach her to forego criticism in the pursuit of contentment. If not happiness, contentment.

"Want a sip of this?"

She floats over to me. The tub is deep. She's a minnow. She perches her lip on the edge of my glass.

"Take it," I say, handing her the wine.

Her pale lips stain crimson. Her face crinkles like a peony. We are alone, together.

"What do you think?" I ask. "Is it what you thought it would be like?"

Her hands pull her body away from me along the edge of the tub. "Not quite."

Not *yuck!* Not *ew!* Not *more more more!* Just *not quite.* My daughter.

"Another sip? Take it."

Swimming back toward me, she reaches out to take the glass. Her soapy fingers slip on the porcelain, sending drops of wine floating on the bathwater.

We watch the red float among mountains of bubbles. Underwater her knees squeeze toward one another. She fingers the spots of blood, disappearing them into the water. Goodbye, wine, goodbye, blood, for now, for a few years, yet.

"Look it up when we get out of the tub," I say. "Parmesan."

"It could be a place," she says.

I do not disagree.

In the bay window, her packed pink weekender on her lap, eleven-year-old Chloe sits, ankles crossed. Her back's turned toward the furniture, toward the television, though it does not play. She's shut her eyes. She refuses to watch the street for her father's big black SUV.

"You haven't seen him in two months. Don't you want to go see where your father lives now?"

"I don't," she says, like she has a choice.

From her bag she takes out a book and begins to fake read.

Her eyes are moving too fast for comprehension. This is her safe space, so I never call her out on this trick. I simply say, *Chloe*, in that way, in that voice, so she knows I know she's trying to hide and that I'm trying to find her.

"I refuse," she says.

A black SUV, as if he had kids to cart around, some young ones to protect.

"Your hands are so greasy," she says, taking my hands in hers, holding them on top of her palms, her thumbs forming a bind around my hands.

"It's just lotion," I say. "For work I have to wash my hands so much, you know."

"Can I have some?"

We leave the window, go to my bedroom. From my bed-side table she takes the large plastic dispenser and sits on the edge of my bed. She pats the space next to her.

"Here," she says, rubbing the lotion into the tops of my hands.

"I'll be here when you get back," I say.

"Good."

"Good?" I repeat.

The heaving of the SUV in the drive as the engine shuts.

"Time to go."

"Promise you'll be here."

"I swear." I swore, I swore.

"I can't do it. I can't put it in."

"Don't push it in at an angle. Just push it straight in."

In the living room, Chloe holds the tampon in the air, unwrapped and exposed, its cotton string dangling along her wrist.

"Do you need help?"

Nods, yes, that's a yes.

"Okay," I say. "Go and lay down."

In her bedroom, she lies on the green shag rug, the rug she said she wanted because she wanted to be able to feel the earth against her skin whenever she wanted. While she was stuck in her room studying, she wanted to be able to lie on the rug and imagine the grass between her toes, the sun warming the skin of her forehead. Her idea. She has always been a daydreamer.

I kneel down beside her.

She lets her legs fall open, slightly.

"It'll feel like a lot of pressure," I say. "But just relax. Tensing up doesn't help." The cotton begins to disappear, it does, but glacially.

"Owww," she eeks.

"Almost there."

"Too much pressure. Stop. Stop." Tears are moving across her cheeks. The pressure isn't all that much. It's more about the fear of being entered, a legitimate fear.

"Just breathe," I say.

"I can't I can't just stop." She is crying, her lips trembling. She throws her arms over her face, nodding her head back and forth to wipe her eyes.

"It's in," I say.

We stand up together.

"How long?" she asks. "Will I know how long?"

"Check in a few hours. You'll learn your flow."

"Just pull the string and it'll come out easy?" she says.

"Easy. Don't worry. It'll come out just fine."

She returns to her room, I to my crossword puzzle on the couch.

"A rat's nest?" ten-year-old Chloe asks.

"The back of your head looks like one." I extend the brush toward her.

"I don't care what other people think. Let them think I'm a rat." She tugs at a knot at the side of her crown. Her eyes are fixated on the knot in the mirror, her untamed eyebrows knit in concentration. In her nude training bra she looks naked. Hips, not yet.

"It's not about what other people think, not entirely. It's about self-respect. And you're a woman, so to a certain extent, it will always be a little bit about what other people think."

She taps her head with the paddle and hands me the brush. In my hand, the knots slip away easier. *We have no choice. I'm sorry.*

"One day all neighborhoods will look just like this one," my mother says. "Look at all of this."

1962. We are driving around Catalina Vista, looking at houses. She and I are out on one of our rare occasions alone together. My brothers and sister are still asleep, but if they were awake they would be off doing teenage things, not spending time with Mom the Realtor and little sis. It is summer and I am out of school. It is very early morning, the sun new over the Rincon. The heat has not yet arrived. By nine, we will be back inside, back in the air-conditioning, back in front of the TV. I am rubbing sleep from my eyes, trying to be as awake as her.

"Everything is in the place it should be. See how all of these houses are one story?" Circling the roundabout, she puts the cigarette between her lips. "That's so you can see the mountains."

Still, the neighborhood is free of human noise, human hustle and bustle. Cottontails are out eating their breakfasts, nibbling on mesquite leaves and cacti and scraps of lettuce left out by the odd beneficent homeowner. The mourning doves coo, enjoying their stage while they have it.

Slowly, though, we see lights go on in windows. The neighborhood is waking up to its sedated wife, its stranger husband, its hungry children, its soiled laundry, its unwashed dishes, a new day of familiar problems and excitements, though at this age, I am only familiar with the disappointments of a child, which are many.

She stops the car on the edge of a small park. Across the street a still-dark house sits hidden behind a row of hairy mountain mahogany. From behind the house, the erect stem of a saguaro seems to protrude right out of its flat white roof. "You want to try?" She holds the cigarette out to me. "Your sister isn't allowed but why the hell not."

Our interactions have the force of an audition. One childish remark and it will give her a reason to love me less. I am eleven and I take the cigarette, put it to my girlish lips, press the cigarette against my skin just enough to taste the nicotine. It is not quite smoking, but I hope that she sees I am trying. I will not smoke, really, until high school, when I date a boy named Peter so that when he goes outside I will not be alone with his friends, people who look at me and do not talk to me, who walk around me like I'm one of those cigar store Indians forced to inhale the smoke. I hand the cigarette back to her, taking care not to upset the balance of ash on the tip, to avoid sending soot onto her white pants. "Do you have any houses here?"

She takes a long drag, her eyes soft, sleepy without makeup. Her thin sun-yellow blond hair is hidden under a blue scarf, yet to be blow dried, curled, Aqua Netted—the possessor of vinyl chloride, the chemical that will seep into her body and grow in her liver as cancer. She will die when I am back home for medical school but she will die in the night while I am sleeping a rare night of sleep. This day, when we are alone, together, is as vulnerable as I will ever see her. "No. Not selling any here. Let's walk a bit."

I do not mention that we are blocking nearly half the road with her car. I get out and follow her across the freshly planted grass of the park. Beneath the towering palm trees, strangers to this desert, we also look like strangers. Our bodies do not enter the other's orbit. We do not hold hands. I do not lean into her skirt when a feeling of affection arises. My hair is black and my skin is brown and her hair is golden and her skin is white. In her cigarette pants she looks like an angel performing an act of charity, outfitting a poor Navajo in a nice dress and showing her what it is like to be a normal child, a loved child, for a day.

In the center of the park there is a bench but we do not

sit on it. A single slide has been placed here for children. No monkey bars. No seesaw. Just a block of gravel with a slide. She does not ask if I want to slide down it because I am too old for such fun and, besides, I don't want to slide down it either. I want to stand by her side, two strangers that happen to be mother and daughter. We walk separately but at the same pace, straight through the park.

It is a small park, so it does not take more than five minutes to get to the other side, to where grass meets pavement. "I'm not ready to go home yet, are you?" she asks, and I say no, I'd like to stay a bit longer. She places her hand on my head, tucking my thick, coarse hair behind my ear, leaving her hand there for a moment longer than I ever thought possible. A mourning dove coos somewhere above our heads.

We begin walking in the direction of the car. My mother stops at the bench. She sits, crossing one leg over the other and taking the pack of cigarettes from her pants pocket, signaling that we are pausing here for a moment. I go to the slide. I am nearly tall enough to reach halfway up the ladder to the top, and I place my hand on each rung, moving my girlish, not-quite-child, not-quite-woman's body up to the top. The slide slides down and out in front of me, a tongue licking the ground, tasting what is to come. I tuck my head to fit under the mouth of the slide and unfold my skinny legs onto the metal. I no longer need to close my eyes like I did when I was younger, when I was too afraid to acknowledge the potential dangers ahead. Now I keep my eyes open, looking not down but out across the green of the park, past the car my mother and I rode here in together, past the armless saguaro and the flat white roof, over the Catalina foothills, past the peak of Mount Lemmon, over the Pacific to an island I know from the space of a crib in the arms of another white angel with yellow socks. I am falling and she is clapping for me.

Dining Room

Tito, what do you think of this wallpaper? I have been looking at a lot of decorating websites lately and even buying those home and garden magazines with the happy white people on the cover, and they seem to be telling me that wallpaper is a thing again. I remember stripping it with my mother in our dining room as a child, the smell of old glue oozing back to life. Back then, no one wanted wallpaper. This was the late nineties, and we were stripping off what the women in the eighties did to their dining rooms, which was to paper it all over with ugly floral bouquets tied off with ribbon.

"No one else is going to do this but you and me," my mother said. "It has to be done. Don't look at me like that. You know I have allergies and I won't survive with all this goldenrod."

Burnt fingertips. After a day of scraping wallpaper we would sit in front of the TV while I held a bag of frozen peas between my hands. *Here*, she'd say, and I would lean over, opening my mouth to grab the spoon of ice cream that we shared from a tub that sat between us.

Bachelard said we have both palace moments and cottage moments. It all depends on the day and the temperature outside and one's mood and the quality of light. Today, I am having a palace moment. I want a chandelier with many crystals that hang over a big Henredon table, a Poliform sofa, an armchair upholstered in pink velvet. I want to stripe the walls in gold. Better yet, I will hire the most expensive painters in town to use the most expensive paints infused with flakes of gold. A queen doesn't lay the marble tiles in her own foyer.

Of course, my palace moments are impossible. I will never be able to afford the one-hundred-dollar-a-gallon paint, the four-hundred-and-fifty-dollar dog bed. I've been dreaming about this ideal home that will never be since I was a child. But, Bachelard says, that's probably for the best. A daydream of elsewhere should be left open at all times.

"For a house that was final, one that stood in symmetrical relation to the house we were born in, would lead to thoughts—serious, sad thoughts—and not to dreams. It is better to live in a state of impermanence than in one of finality."

This is how I will make this home happen: Pat bought me out of the our-house and then gave me a lump sum, for the remodeling, the new furniture buying, the purchasing of spices, cleaning supplies, linens, to replace the ones from our life together. The lump sum was generous. Too generous. I wish he had left me standing in the driveway of this empty house, not even a Swiffer to wipe up my new, lonely messes.

But he didn't. His contribution will keep me renovating the kitchen, the master bath. I could build a deck and still have something left over to refinish the hardwood floors. He left me in a position whereby I couldn't harbor even a modicum of anger toward him. Accruing resentment like trying to climb a greased pole to the moon.

Some houses have names but the one Pat and I owned didn't and this one doesn't either. Beau says we no longer name our houses because we move around so much. If we were to name these places, we would have too much difficulty in letting them go.

Or, I suppose, you could just name every place of residence the same thing, like how someone would name all the dachshunds of their lives Eleanor. You disappear the loss under a facade of continuity. Eleanor and Eleanor and Eleanor.

"We should have registered," my twenty-six-year-old self told Pat. "Then we would never have gotten these plates. These are an affront to the eye."

Against the light coming in through the bay window, he held up the plate, examining its floral detailing. "It's not so bad. We can't really afford anything else right now."

This was our starter-rental home. All containable, manageable spaces and corners.

Then, everything with us was justs. Just twenty-six, just married, just moved to a new town, which depleted our individual bank accounts, even with the assistance of his parents, just the two of us now, with an assortment of expensive plates and cutlery and vases and no cash for the pizza man. We felt lucky for what we had. But I still hated the plates. And the Formica table with the rusted legs that was trendy but made us a cliché of young married life. We were just like those young people who loved things that were falling apart because they didn't know anything about what it actually meant, what it actually felt like, for things and people to fall apart.

"One day when we are settled and can afford it we will buy plates that you want," my young husband said.

"It doesn't matter," I said. "I'm being stupid. They are just plates."

"Nothing is stupid about plates."

In our new kitchen we fucked and talked of a puppy.

Part of building a house necessitates living in denial that it could ever fall apart.

On the hillside behind the house we laid a blanket, and I picked some flowers and placed them down between us. I had cooked eggs and apple sausage and he had pressed fresh orange juice. It was the first day of spring and it was just warm enough to be out in the morning air again.

He brought the plate to meet his knee, sending shards of porcelain across the grass.

"What are you doing?" I asked, rubbing my cheek with the heel of my hand, erasing a granule of bread into my skin.

"So we are committed to a future of new plates," he said. "We will have the plates that we want."

The thighs of his jeans were streaked with egg yolk. I took my empty glass and pitched it across the field of tall grasses and wildflowers that spread before us. He pulled the red blanket around us. The weight of his body pressed my nose into the earth and I could taste the sweetness of oranges.

While I eat, I listen to the police scanner. I discovered an app that you could download onto your cell phone, providing access to the feeds of police departments across the country, from Boise to Miami.

Over breakfast I sit cross-legged on the floor and set the phone down next to my plate. My go-to stations include the Las Vegas Metropolitan Police, Detroit Police Dispatch, and Salt Lake City PD. Every now and then I will choose randomly, listening into a suburb of Kansas or a strip of desert highway outside of Reno. The officers' voices are muffled. I chew quietly, so I can make out the words. I have to train my ear. I have to learn the codes.

He 401-ed into another car meaning the perp drove his car into another person's vehicle, causing an accident. *Pancake. Paper bitch. Pep rally alley.* I like learning this jargon, which makes me feel close to these stranger-professionals in their pressed uniforms. Through this shared language, I feel a connection, however tenuous, to the female officer driving to a taco shop where a man has been reported throwing himself into the walls of a bathroom around nine in the morning.

As I spoon cereal into my mouth, a cop in Reno is already hours into his shift. I imagine him rising in the dark, buttoning his uniform, kissing his wife on the cheek (who is still fast asleep, whose alarm won't go off for another three hours), and driving off into the dark morning. Maybe he stopped to get a coffee, but it's likely he didn't have time. Someone is having an allergic reaction to a medication on the other side of town. In so many ways, he is needed.

At the scene, he rolls down the squad car's window, the air cold and stiff, which he cuts with cigarette smoke. He rolls up the window, pauses, smiles.

It is so much easier to keep a house clean without any furniture. The Shakers were also well aware of this fact. They hung their chairs upside down on their walls to prevent dust from accumulating on their seats, to more swiftly sweep their handcrafted wood floors. Maybe I'll keep this room like this. Empty, with just the light through the window for shapeliness. That's all I need for now.

At a later date, maybe I'll feel the impulse to buy a solid wood chair that is overpriced but whose beautifully carved details I won't be able to resist. I will put it in the corner by the window and listen to Reno, cereal bowl on my lap.

Fuck dining tables. I'll eat on the floor, on a red blanket with white plates.

Kitchen

From a blog post on the application of color psychology to the home:

RED: Beware of red in the kitchen, especially if you are watching your waistline: red triggers the gut. Side effects of red kitchen walls: snacking and overeating. Save red for the workout room, as red increases your blood pressure and heart rate, kicking your ass into gear.

GREEN: Green is the color of focus. Save this hue for the rooms of the mind, the home office, for example. The mind thrives in *Frosted Emerald*.

BLUE: Lose weight with blue. It can curb your appetite. Or it can lower your heart rate and make you more productive. Blue. All the rooms of the world should be blue.

WHITE: Convey cleanliness with white. Beware of its sterilizing effects. Use white to sanitize the areas that need it most, the areas that need to be purged of demons—dust or mind-natured—the bathroom, the kitchen, maybe even the bedroom, the hall closet, the living room. White, for this time of my life. Not a sign of purity, but of mourning, as in Hindu culture. Save the reds for occasions of love and triumph, weddings and Holi.

On the five-year anniversary of my father's leaving us, my mother and I did girl things. In a freshly steamed dress with horizontal stripes that maximized the width of her breasts and hips, she waited at the base of the steps of the school bus.

"I want my hair to look like yours." I stopped at her feet, fingering the rubber band tied around the muddled ochre strands lying on my shoulder.

"You want to have more fun, is that it?" She turned her head, creating a portrait profile, gussying her perfect blond bob that no one would care too much about, not the other doctors and certainly not her patients with their legs spread before her. Maybe a nurse offered a kind word or two now and then, asking for a recommendation for a colorist in town. Surely they must have craved that perfect blond bob, which was in no way natural but nevertheless illuminated the gold in her muddy skin. "Hop in. We're going to Sally's."

Two girls riding to the beauty store. This was our anniversary. No boys allowed.

As a child, I wrote the following on the cardboard interior of my school notebook's back cover:

> *How many girls have cried into the soup*
> *How many girls have cried into the spaghetti sauce*
> *At least two, at least two*

- Cotton
- China White
- Honeymilk
- Great White
- Lily of the Valley
- Decorator's White
- Paper White
- White Whisp
- Oyster
- Winter Orchard
- Swiss Coffee
- Slipper Satin
- White Dove
- Chantilly Lace
- Greek Villa
- WL-05
- Gypsum
- White Chocolate

- White Tie
- Linen
- Pointing

I'm imagining the conversations that will take place at the hypothetical dining room table when people come to visit. Like my mother, for instance, who lives a two-ish hour drive away, in a suburb outside of D.C. At some inevitable point, she will come and visit.

"There's something wrong with that dog," she will say.

"How do you mean?"

"He's pacing all over the place. Doesn't he lay down? Isn't that what dogs are supposed to do?" she'll ask. "Lay down?"

She forbid me to have a pet when I was growing up. *Unsanitary* was the word she used.

"He has anxiety and won't eat," I'll say.

"Don't we all."

"He's on Prozac."

"And? Does that make him special?" Then she will bring a porcelain cup very delicately to her lips, because she won't drink her coffee in anything else but this paper-thin china, and sip in a way that you can't hear her swallow. It is rude, she used to say, to make noises when you eat. She is a preserver of silence, one of the last of the kind left in this country. I've come to appreciate this quality.

"I can't remember what you told me, but what do they have Pat on for nausea? Zofran? Anzemet? Aloxi?"

"How the hell would I know," I'll say, pushing my chair away from her, and I will rant about how many times I've told her that I don't know what kind of pills he's on, that he isn't speaking to me, that I know nothing, that he may not even need the pills anymore because he is better, or it's too late.

The crystal rattling in the hypothetical cabinet, I'll say, *I know nothing.*

$1.99 for a set of Snow White Matte Ceramic Subway Tile. A set includes forty pieces, total. The weight of the set is 33.37 pounds, precisely. A single tile is approximately four inches by twelve inches.

Marry the Snow White Matte Ceramic Subway Tile with the complementary Pure White Matte Hexagonal Porcelain Tile for a chic, unified look throughout your space. This unique Subway Tile will make you the envy of all your friends. Be careful with this tile—its sheen of perfection will be off-putting to some, who cannot financially or emotionally afford the Snow White Matte Ceramic Subway Tile. Be prepared to lose friends, who will find that the perfect kitchen you have created reflects on the shoddiness of their own kitchens, and by extrapolation, their lives. The Snow White Matte Subway Tile is an indispensable component to the perfect home. Don't forego this exquisite detail. Your idyllic life will be disconcerting to others.

An anthropologist, for the purpose of a study on the union of couples' routines, visited a recent widow in her home. Sitting at the kitchen table, the widow, the anthropologist noticed, had bruises on her forehead.

"He used to shut the cabinet doors," the widow said, the impressions on her forehead the same shades of blue eyeshadow drag queens and preteens paint on their eyelids, as if she wanted to prove something to strangers. "I didn't even know I left them open."

The mailwoman has not arrived, though it is three thirty, her usual drop-off hour. I peek through the window, but I do not see her truck or her blues, which she fills out in all the right places, making the uniform look stylish, even kind of sexy, her jet-black hair falling in waves down the middle of her back.

I run to the driveway and get in the car. With my head out the window, I scan the mailboxes, looking for the naked, flaccid semaphore flags. I follow the trail of these particular mailboxes until I reach the vertical flag, erect and proud. I park the car, get out, standing in the middle of the street. I scan the landscape. Children shriek, in the good, fun-having register, a sound that washes over me as if I were underwater and everyone else were dry, looking down on me.

There.

I do not even lock the car door. I run-walk up behind her as she coasts down the sidewalk, earphones shutting her off from the outside world. I can hear her music, some pop-soul song that goes *Baby baby baby*. I put my hand on her shoulder.

She stumbles as she turns around to look at her assailant, tearing a single earphone from her right ear, the strand dangling inept at her breast.

It all made so much sense back at the house. I have scared this woman, all for a package of plates.

In A World of Too Many Options, Here Are Some More: The Countertop Issue

NATURALS

Marble: $50 to $150 per square foot, installed.
  PROS: Glamour, color options, heat resistant. CONS: Coffee stains will kill the dream. Price makes fantasy.
Limestone: $50 to $100 per square foot, installed.
  PROS: Beauty. CONS: Price. Upkeep. Sensitivity. Even tidy people leave stains.
Granite: $40 to $100 per square foot, installed.
  PROS: Low-maintenance, scratch and stain resistant, high resale value. CONS: Oh, Mom.
Butcher Block: $40 to $100 per square foot, installed.
  PROS: Instant cutting board. If you're into the wabi-sabi aesthetic, the wear will be glorious. CONS: High maintenance. You can't unsee my cuts.

ENGINEERED

Corian, Celador, Silestone, Caesarstone.
  PROS: No sealant required, cost effective, low-maintenance, names like knights. CONS: Burns easily.

I thought I saw him. I think I did. That curly head of hair in the passenger seat and my mother driving. Pat and my mother had always been friendly, had shared a comfortable rapport, but. The head of hair and my mother were crossing the intersection. They looked glamorous in their black sunglasses and smiles.

Lost, I tapped the car in front of me. There was a small show. The other driver and I got out of our cars and looked at the bumper. The driver shook his head, endlessly. He never said a word. He just kept shaking his head until he got in his car and drove away.

It's impossible, of course.

Once an Army brat, always an Army brat, my mother likes to say. As a child, due to the nature of my grandfather's work, she and her siblings were picked up and moved around every few years, from Tucson to Stuttgart to Norfolk to Tucson again. This impermanence stunted her sense of home. Her desire to root was less like a dream or aspiration than a craving, a biological imperative. When she had me, she saw this other biological truth, me, as an opportunity to sate the itch for good.

To settle, she and my father chose a cul-de-sac situated on the edge of a pond in an upper-middle-class suburb outside of D.C., among other people who wanted a little peace and quiet to raise their own. It was her chance to finally know a home.

Even when he moved on from us, she stayed, kept the house for herself, for me. After two husbands, she had concluded that men only made home making more difficult. Alone, she could still preserve the fantasy of home.

I know she will die there, in my childhood home, nondescriptly, in a neighborhood where a new set of yearners, dreamers have taken root.

After years of moving around, of willful impermanence, I want to settle, too. I am only now realizing that I am just like her.

* * *

"Two of the small plates shattered and four of the large ones," I tell the customer service woman over the phone. My toes poke out of the bathwater. I practice curling and uncurling them, one by one, a wave building, cresting, breaking, settling, and starting over again. "I will need those replaced."

"How many total plates do you need?"

"I need two more of the small. Four of the large."

"Can you tell me again what happened?" the customer service person asks.

"Like I said, the postal worker has no delicacy. She just drops the boxes on the doorstep like a caveman."

"You mean cavewoman. Are you sure it's her fault?"

"Is this standard protocol, to assume the customer is lying?"

"No, ma'am. However, there is some distress in your voice that makes me think that maybe you're not telling me the whole truth."

"Just because there's distress in my voice doesn't mean I'm lying. I could be under duress for a number of reasons."

"What did you say?"

"I could be under duress for any number of reasons."

"I don't think you're using that word correctly."

"Oh. Well."

"I'm sorry for making things worse. I will send you the six plates."

"It's okay. I understand. I bet people try to con the system all the time."

"You wouldn't believe."

"People must be desperate or something."

"Especially this time of year. The holidays always make people do crazy things."

"I'm remodeling a kitchen that may cost as much as a low-end sedan."

"You must have a good job, ma'am."

"Well, the thing is, my husband, ex-husband, is giving me some money for the house. I'm a freelancer. He has the good job."

"He sounds like a good man. A real good one."

"I would never be able to afford these things on my own. If you only knew how much this fireclay farmhouse sink costs."

"I'm telling you. People do crazy things. But what you're saying is understandable."

"Thank you for saying that. You know, it's just me here. There's not even anyone else in this house with whom I can eat pie on these new plates."

"Someone will come over. Especially if it's good pie."

"Are you sure that's not crazy?"

"Is what crazy?"

"Never mind."

"It's not the craziest thing I've heard today, ma'am. You can bet on that."

"You're good at this. I will make sure to write you a positive review online."

"I appreciate that, ma'am. I will send you the six plates. Is there anything else I can help you with tonight?"

"I'm just getting started but I'll let you go."

"Sleep well, ma'am."

"And you too."

While slicing tomatoes, Pat told me he was sick. The fruits were firm and juicy, beautiful yellow things fresh from our garden.

He felt that, though doctors were cautiously hopeful, he could not be. We had built the garden only a year before, our shared project, a place that could bear fruit for a future generation. He needed to wait his death out alone. Even their skins smelled fragrant. From his private island, our home, he would watch the disease come closer and closer, sitting solo on the shore as the ship puttered into port. The juice, it was so sweet.

What am I supposed to do, I ask friends, strangers, the checkout clerk at the grocery store. I want to send the ship away. I want to destroy its electronic equipment so it cannot know which way it needs to go. I want the ship to disappear, for its captain and crew to never be heard from again.

But I can't do anything like that because I don't know what the ship looks like. Is it a sailboat or an aircraft carrier? Maybe it's not even a ship at all. The cancer is just a fog that has taken the shape of a destroyer.

He told me, we can't stay living here together anymore. We must remember this house in its complete happiness. This decision is for us.

One day I stroke, and M. strokes back. It has been three or four years since we last spoke, since I was last in his bed, since Pat and I had our drifting moment. But the yearning, as always, is still there. We emerge from the cave again, hungry.

I've already chipped two of the plates. I'm awaiting the first glass to break like the ball drop on New Year's Eve. I'm trying to be more honest, so I've decided on the butcher block. Let the nicks of my knife proliferate.

Downstairs Hall Closet

You can't forget the small spaces. Do not neglect the corner of the living room, the third shelf in the hall closet adjacent to the half bath. These require your attention as much as the master bed and the color of the walls in the baby's room, if there is a baby.

A plant. Put a plant in the corner. Something leafy and green that will remind you of the tropics, of somewhere not here. Drape a sheepskin imported from Reykjavik on the delicate chair by the foyer window. In those moments of despair, you can look at that plant or sheepskin and think of elsewhere, of a beach on an island that may or may not exist. Like God or the Resurrection, it doesn't matter what part is real, what actually happened. You don't need to believe in it for its powers to work. That plant will save you.

Think of your corners. These places make a difference.

* * *

This was my thinking when I was a child: toss all of Mom's shoes into the closets, under the bed. Take her coats from off the arm of the sofa and from the backs of the chairs and shove them in there, too. Close all the cupboards that she has left ajar. Turn off the faucet she has left running, in the kitchen, in the bathroom, downstairs, and upstairs.

I'd shove all of my mother's messes into the closet. Whatever I could fit. If someone were to come over, which they never did—my mother never had visitors—they would think everything was perfect.

"We are going for a drive," Beau says over the phone. Beau, a sculptor and professor, a graduate school roommate, confidant, grocery gatherer. Now he teaches at a local university. He lives alone in an apartment above a hardware store that he will never let me see. "You need to get out of the house."

In his hulking white F-150, the bed and rear cab packed with bolts of tulle and polypropylene netting, he drives us around the green hills that distinguish the central terrain of the state. The air is warm maybe for the last time this year. Soon, it will be full-bore winter. The changing of the seasons now happens in an instant.

He packs a picnic of stinky cheese and hard crackers and good bourbon. He is good at these things.

"Doesn't the air feel nice? Doesn't it feel right out here?" He takes a cut of home-sliced cheese from a Pyrex container, places it on a cracker, and hands it to me.

Around us, people with kids and dogs jump out of cars and scurry into a nondescript brick building. We are picnicking at a rest stop.

"Virginia has the most beautiful rest stops of any state," he says. "Except Mississippi. If only you could visit one of those rest stops. You'd never want to leave."

He tells me he fantasizes often about these travelers. He says you can look at them and consider what they are wearing, listen to the cadence of their voices and accents and wonder where they are going, under what circumstances, to a wedding or a funeral or back home for a holiday. He watches the woman in her twenties walking her dog along the designated area of grass just for pets. He admires the trucker stretched out on the soft hill, his cap tipped down over his eyes and the top of his shirt unbuttoned so that the sun can warm and rejuvenate him for another thousand miles.

Beau likes to think about these people temporarily without homes. "Like fish out of a tank," he says. "Some are awkward because they are learning what freedom really means." *Learn from them*, he wants to say to me, though he doesn't. *Look at their faces.*

My husband chose this house. While we tended our garden, he said, "I found you a house you will love."

In the last month of our life together, we drove from our house to my new house for the inspection. Together, not together, we walked room by room, following the inspector, who had the habit of pulling up his too-loose jeans by the front of his belt. Pat brought along his friend, a builder of spec homes, to assess what improvements could be made.

"These beams aren't bearing," Pat's friend, Carl, said, pointing at a piece of wood hovering over the master bedroom.

"So you can raise the ceiling here. You really don't want these low ceilings."

Walking downstairs, he'd point at a wall along the banister and say, "Knock it out." There were a few walls to knock out.

Surveying the water filtration system, Pat pointed at a bright blue vessel.

"That's for soft water," Carl said.

"Meaning?" I said.

"It converts hard water into soft water. Soft water's easier on the pipes. And it doesn't leave any splotchy shit on glasses. I have it in my house."

"What's the downside?" I ask.

"Sometimes you feel like you can't get the soap off."

"That's not good," Pat said, talking to but not looking at me.

"It's not true," Carl said. "It's actually better at getting the soap off. It's just most people are used to hard water and think that *squeaky* feeling means you're clean. It's bullshit. That's a layer of soap scum on you."

"Interesting," Pat said, looking at me.

"We were never actually clean," I said, clarifying things for us all.

After the inspector left, we stood around the kitchen island, assessing.

"I'd say this house is ninety percent there," Carl said, hands resting atop the laminate, definitely-in-need-of-replacing countertop.

"That's good news, then?" I asked.

"Great news," Pat said. "So most of the renovations are fun, cosmetic, nothing structural, right?"

"Mostly fun, yeah," Carl affirmed.

Fun.

This closet is the only part of the house that doesn't need updating, painting, refinishing, rewiring. Whoever lived here before had kept this closet in pristine condition. He, she, they, had painted the space an eggshell white that radiates. Its glossy finish emits an odor of chemical purity. The odor has yet to be tainted by the muskiness of dust motes. I fold the towels and extra set of linens and blankets and set them onto the shelves. I flick the switch and the bulb illuminates just as it should, providing the kind of light that's warm and yellow and terrible for the environment.

Look, Tito. Wonderful.

Guest Room

I am jumping from room to room. Downstairs and now upstairs.
I am avoiding certain spaces. I am not ready for them yet.

Le Corbusier would be upset with me. Without a plan, he
would say, you have willfulness. You have no order.

I have become a magnet for chaos.

Aside from the au pairs, no one ever stayed in my mother's
guest room. The only people to filter in and out of our lives
were the service people, those who came to deliver the mail,
repair the kitchen sink, check the water heater.

"Do you know what the ruelle is?" my mother said over
breakfast the morning after she discovered me, for the first
time, fast asleep in the crevice between the bed and the wall
of the guest room, a blanket draped over my body, toes pok-
ing out from beneath.

Ruelle. She liked to hear the word break from her lips.
While raising me, in the few spare hours she had, she dug into

her history, learning French, Japanese, the things her adoptive parents had never shared with her. Her learning, inevitably, meant that I, too, would learn. She wanted me to know that she, and by extension, me, did not belong to some Waspy vision of America. Our house could never be surrounded by a white picket fence, a nice and clean family of four tucked inside. That experience was not for us.

"A ruelle," she continued, "is what you were asleep in." She sipped at the edge of her coffee cup, as if the liquid were still hot. We had already been sitting at the table for an hour, a ritual she set out for us every Saturday morning, learning our heritage. "De quoi as-tu peur?" she asked.

I shrugged my shoulders, followed the cereal in my milk.

"What are you afraid of?"

I had an "A" and an "L" and an "O," but I also had an "F" and a "U" and a "T." I had a "B" and another "O" and a "Y." I had many letters. I was just getting started.

"If it makes you feel better, then you can sleep down there," she said, standing from the table, our lesson over for the day. "Just don't forget to bring a pillow. Make it cozy. Make it yours."

Beau loves men and women but he has never loved me, in that erotic way.

"We both know you are untouchable," he says when I ask him, for probably the tenth time in our lives, why he has never felt anything close to a sexual tinge around me, when he has seen my breasts and my eyes made up into those of cat's and my lips rouged matte and intending. Though he has also (accidentally) run his fingers along unshaven armpits, (intentionally) rubbed his nose along the underarm of my T-shirt.

"What does that mean?"

"You have never been quite real to men." He cuts the donut in half on the butcher block. He holds the sweetness to my mouth. "You're very easy to turn into a concept."

"You think I'm a concept?"

"Of course not. I'm just speaking about most men."

We are up late painting. Our wrists, our necks, our cheeks, are streaked with white. Primer. We are priming. After an evening of whiskey and painting, we both agree that it is best that he sleep here tonight. In the guest room, I make up a bed for him, which is really just a twin-sized air mattress lying on the floor. "Is this good enough?"

He lies down on top of the mattress, his slacks and paint-speckled T-shirt and uniform Chuck Taylors still on. "When have I ever told you you're not enough?" He removes a shoe and tosses it to me. I throw it back at him, harder than I meant, hitting him square in the chest with a soft thud.

My body is hot. I remove my raggedy knit sweater and throw it at him. I have been dreaming of sex, waking in the morning with my legs knit together in longing, not for anyone in particular but for everyone. For Pat, but also for M. and the man at the coffee shop with the wife and baby at her nipple.

Beau folds the sweater on his lap, tucking the arms so carefully, as if they held my own fragile limbs. We have never slept together and likely never will, and that, we both agree, is a good thing. But he understands what I'm going through, and he is considerate of my vain desiring.

"Try to rest," he says.

I nod, backing out of the room in my thinning camisole, breasts sunken like cowering dogs. I shut out the light from the room.

Rome Rome Rome Rome Rome

I pinch the skin all up and down my arms. I pinch the skin of my eyelids. I pinch my kneecaps and my toes and pull the hairs on my ankles. I poke my ass and slap my stomach.

A psychiatrist on the radio told an anecdote: A girl in his ward was always taking glass or whatever she could find and cutting herself with it. After many times of her doing this, he threatened her, "This time, I will not use anesthesia to sew you up!"

She laughed. "Don't you see that I do this because I am trying to feel, that I cannot feel anything at all?"

I wake up the next morning with bruises, little knots of pain tied into my skin.

Dreams. I've never remembered them, but suddenly I'm swimming in their remnants.

I have been dreaming of a shack on a beach in a tropical spot of sea. The boards that make up its walls are bowed, providing small windows that peek out onto the interminable ocean. The roof is wood, too, I think, sturdy, leakless. It's more like a cabin you'd see in the Yukon than in Lahaina. In my dreams, I am always there alone, sitting on the sand floor of the shack. But water never gets in. Whoever thought to build it knew how far back from the shoreline the shack had to be. This is supposed to be a safe place.

Always, right before I wake up into the noise of real life, I am falling asleep to the sound of small waves rolling out onto the beach. At the moment of quiet that exists before the next wave, I open my eyes. Dream silence meets waking silence. This has become my favorite part of the day.

In the old house, I am vomiting. We are having company—my mom is visiting—and I am vomiting. A stomach bug. A bad bite of chicken. Something is preventing me from being a good host. But Pat steps in.

"You need to rest," Pat says, ushering me up the stairs, away from the dinner table, from conversation, from life.

"We will be okay," my mother says. "We will save some wine for you."

"That's not true at all." My body is being led away from me. Pat's hands are doing all the work. My own legs, arms, are weightless, worthless. On the way to our room, we pass the guest room. The door is open. My mother's sweater is laid out across the bed, just in case. My body is hot, my skin insulating when it should be cooling. A cold bath, maybe. But no, he's leading me to bed, to rest.

"I will bring you some water and a cold washcloth for your forehead," he says, tucking me in. I kick off the sheets like a child.

"You need to rest." He puts his hands on both sides of my

head. He does not recoil against the heat of my skin. He moves his hand across the topography of my face, sensing, feeling for answers. He does not panic. "Listen to us. We know what's best."

Off the lights go. Away he goes, the door closing behind him, shutting me into the room. The stairs creak as he leaves me. My mother's laugh, jubilant when it comes, pushes up against the bedroom floor. Wine leaves the bottle, I know it. I feel it going.

Le Corbusier offered this wisdom: "A house is a machine for living in." But machines break, become defunct, outdated. Certain parts wear out from use. Sometimes, these machines stop working and you can never say why, what the cause is. To the non-mechanically minded, we will never know what's wrong.

Or sometimes machines break and we know exactly what happened. We can point to the exact knob or wire or leg of the chair that is in disrepair. But it is too late for the machine. Nothing can be done to elevate it to its original, functioning state. It no longer constitutes a chair, with its three legs. The machine has become something else entirely, something unrecognizable and foreign and cold. The machine must be abandoned.

Our house was a machine for happiness.

Kire-tsuzuki. Cut-continuance. In aesthetics, the idea of some element that at once halts events in space or time and bridges forward. A lily cut from the garden, now dying, becomes even more radiant in the vase, its true nature, its impermanence, revealed. The lily is, as Nishitani says, "like a person who has eradicated all attachments to life and abandoned all expectations fundamental to our mundane existence." The cut flower "transcends the constructs of time and signifies a movement into new life as a moment."

In his sleep he is like a little boy, a streak of white paint on his cheek, his mouth ajar, hair ruffled. The air mattress's slow leak of air doesn't bother him. Beau sleeps like the dead, like the young. His sneakers lay adrift as if kicked off in sleep, the laces inching across the floor like caterpillars. They say it is easy to convert a guest room into a guest room/nursery. Simply use transitional fabrics that are appealing to adult and baby alike. Situate a day bed against one wall and a crib against the other. Paint the ceiling with vivid patterns for stimulation. Balance out any whimsical details with sleek, modern furniture. Design the room as a place of possibility.

Master Bath

My skin feels off. I am slick. If someone tried to rub their hand on my arm, they would slide right over me, over my skin and away from me. I rub and rub, scratch and scratch, trying to get the slickness off of me.

I try to tell myself that I am cleaner now, that this is an improvement. I try to think of the soap scum around the shower drain in the other house. I tell myself, the water here is *softer*, less harsh, not as abrasive. But still, I itch. I itch.

Who would have thought that a change in the texture of the skin, a smoothening, could be so maddening? I scrub and scrub.

This morning, I hold the lipstick in my hand and apply it to my lips, but I keep drawing outside the lines, so unlike a child's unconscious scribblings, with no joy in my mistakes. The red wanders off my upper lip like it's got much better things to do, like it has no business living where society says the color should live.

Today is an unusual day, one in which a client from D.C. is in town and suggests meeting for a friendly, casual lunch. Which means I must make myself up. I must brush my hair in the way that clients prefer, slicked and smooth and even around my face, like a doll. I must present myself as someone employable, someone capable of producing content that presents their brands as respectable business entities.

This is not the work I had planned for myself as a young English major enthralled with Keats and Blake, but it is fine. This work gives me flexibility. How many people can say that they can design their days around their own wants, whims, and needs? I am lucky.

In the mirror I see that I should not lock myself away. It is not unfeasible that someone would find me worth taking out to dinner, worth fucking, lipstick or not.

With an alcohol-soaked Q-tip, I clean up the lines. I stick my forefinger between my lips and slide it out, as some mothers teach their daughters, lining my knuckle with a halo of red, soon to be washed away in the foam of the tap.

I am a woman. I must paint within the lines.

After our workdays finished, Pat and I entered into a ritual. The bath was our moment of coming together, of union, our disparate days converging at this point in the house, upstairs above the downstairs hall closet, in the spot adjacent to our bedroom, where this ritual would terminate. Unlike me he worked a traditional job that required sport coats and office hours. These things needed to be washed away, just as my computer screen eyes needed to be cleansed.

Into the center of the basin he'd lower himself, cold porcelain on warm skin, and I'd start filling, and he would always say, *Make it hotter*, knowing that I liked the water scalding, and I'd turn the heat up higher but not as hot as I would have wanted it to be, and then I'd perch behind him on the ledge of the tub, my thighs a vise around his torso, the soles of my feet scrubbing his legs, exfoliating the day off of his skin, our legs reddening rapidly in the hot soak. Over the peaks of his shoulders that protruded out of the water, our shared sea, I'd empty cups of water, my hands skimming bathwater like we were in a faulty boat filling fast, the ocean overtaking us, our schooner sinking, and I was responsible for saving us, naked me, without a plug, without the gills for breathing underwater.

After, he'd lift me off the back of the basin and pull me by the hand to the bedroom, to the bed. Dampening the sheets, we'd eventually fall asleep, on a bed sudsy and cold.

"How many lightbulbs do we need?" Pat and I walked through the automatic doors of Lowe's.

"Four, I think," I said. "No. Five. Five bulbs."

"Are you sure?"

"Of course. You're always asking if I'm sure. Can't you have faith in my sureness?"

The aisles shone a greasy blue. They must have been freshly soaked and sudsed the night before, not yet to be tarnished by garden-soiled boots. That Sunday morning, the aisles were spare, possessing a holy quietude.

"Blink," he said. "There's something in your eye."

We paused in the intermediate space between the aisles and the registers, out in the open. I blinked.

"I can't feel anything."

"I'm telling you," he said. "It's there."

"It's not. I feel fine. The eye is fine."

"Dear."

It was just like my mother said it would be. Like pulling off a Band-Aid, she said, taking some skin with it. How did she know what it would be like to tell him about M., I asked, since she had never strayed in either of her marriages? True, she said, but her patients would tell her stories. From their experiences, she said, neglecting to mention her own intimacy with being strayed upon, she understood the quality of that particular strain of pain.

The orientation of the skin of his eyes and cheeks and lips did not register as anger. He said, *I understand. I understand. I understand*, over and over. That repetition. *I understand. I understand. I understand.*

The lightbulbs.

Four or five.

One for the lamp on the table by the bed. Two for the lamps in the downstairs living area. One for the floor lamp in my office. One extra bulb, just in case.

This is a sacred place. If I said any more I'd tear the tender mystery of it. But to give a slightly rounder impression, to add a little more fullness to your understanding but not enough to burst, it's like this: Imagine the happiest of your personal rituals. It's not about any period of extended contentedness in your life, but the habitual, iterable moments of contained joy that slow time. Maybe it's sitting on the couch and watching British murder mysteries with your cat, your feet soaking in a paraffin bath. Maybe it's walking in the woods with your aging mother, holding hands, smoking a shared cigarette as the winter air reddens the corresponding apples of your cheeks. For me, it's our moments in the bath. Enough.

"All rooms have four walls, a door, a window or two, a bed, a chair, and perhaps a bidet," Jean Rhys wrote in *Good Morning, Midnight*. "A room is a place where you hide from the wolves outside and that's all any room is."

Beau

Out on the town we are Bonnie and Clyde. We are bitches, troublemakers, outlaws. We talk too loudly at restaurants. We laugh at children falling on the sidewalk. We hold hands and dance on street corners, even when there is no music, because there is no music. We are just as inclined to make it ourselves.

In Chloe's house we are something else altogether. Not lovers, but something deeper and more stable.

"Pass me the magazine," she says, her arm materializing from out behind the transparent shower curtain liner. In the new house, she has yet to buy a substantial cloth curtain. This is not because she lacks for money. In addition to what Pat has given her, she has her own source of income. She is a savvy person and long ago figured out how to use words to coerce, sell, provide her a living that doesn't require her to go to an office and follow someone else's orders. She is not rich—her earnings lay in writing, after all—but she is no freeloader either. She can afford the curtain. Simply put, the naked shower curtain liner is part of her avoidance, another component of dealing with all that has happened.

"But we're talking," I say, sitting on top of a stack of unfolded towels piled atop the toilet seat.

"We are not talking. You are talking and I am letting you talk."

"Then tell me something. Tell me who this man is you're going out with this week."

"Some architect from the internet."

"Architects are some of the most neurotic people I know. Why would you subject yourself to an architect?"

"He speaks four languages. He designs buildings for a living. It could be a productive relationship."

"If you're going to sleep with him, I don't want to know the details."

She throws the curtain open and tosses a cupped hand of water in my direction. On the floor around my ankles, miniature pools of soapy bathwater settle like lily pads. This is new for us, this shared bath time, since she has been alone in the new house, since Pat has sequestered himself inside their house, since she has started over.

But our playing is not entirely new. For the entirety of our relationship, this has been a game of ours. We raise flags of passion that turn out to be just shadows. Through repeated trial and error, we're discovering that we want nothing of the other's wetness.

In the bath a patchwork of bubbles frame her breasts like scales on a fish. Her limbs are lithe and translucent, her veins swimming blue against the edges of her skin. She is one of those people that doesn't seem to fit on this earth, where CPAs hover in cubicles and cell phones yawp about war and the latest technological upgrade. I let her know that I see her, that her otherness is seen.

I've often wondered how nice it would be, though, if the shadows turned out to have substance.

"Excuse me," she says. "What are you thinking? Your eyes glazed over. Is this too weird?"

"It's not weird at all," I assure her.

"I'm getting out though." She pulls the curtain closed around her. "It's not a date," she adds. "I met him at a Denny's, not online," as if that clarifies things. "Just friends."

I pick up a wrinkled towel from beneath my seat and extend a hand into the shower curtain. I do not look.

She pulls the curtain open. A smile attempts to pull her lips up over her teeth. She is learning happiness again. She turns off the water.

We are like an old country-western duo, lovers or siblings, sometimes it's hard to tell which with those couples. They both share that same glowing head of hair and set of long eyelashes to bat at the camera. Which we do. We do a lot of lash batting at one another, at waiters and bar-backs when we're out together. Flirting: another ritual.

In her new solitude, we have become closer, our two bubbles of consciousness pressing up against one another. We are like conjoined twins, Chloe and I.

"Chloe, I'm coming over."

"I'm really busy here. I'm painting. I'm elbow deep in paint. I'm getting white all over my phone. Are you going to buy me a new phone?"

"When will you be done painting? Will you let me come over then? Actually, I don't care. I'm coming over anyway."

"You can't just come over whenever you feel like it," she says. "You know that, don't you?"

"I know that I'm coming over. How long has it been since you left the house?"

"I left for groceries."

"When was that?" I prod. "Last month?"

"Three days ago, actually."

"Put on a clean shirt. I'm taking you out."

"You're a pain in my ass."

"I love you, you know that," I say.

Without hesitation, she says, "I love you, too."

I hear her sigh, hear her exhaling past the dead phone line, her solitude escaping mine, her bubble bouncing away from me.

We are Cash and Carter, except we've never shared the same bed.

"Sculpture is the art of control freaks," I tell my students. "It is the art of people who feel the world pulling away from them. Sculpting comes from an irrational need to shape a reality that is incapable of being shaped."

The kids sign up for my art history classes in droves. Aside from the art students, the econ majors especially take a liking to my course. They all think I know something, that I have some secret about the world that I'm going to divulge in this fifty-minute class in this generic lecture hall situated in the hills of old Virginia.

Despite what the students believe, every teacher knows that we are just making it up as we go along.

If I know that it's all a sham, then how do I have the confidence to unload all of this pseudo-philosophical shit on them? All I can say is that, over the years, the words have leaked out of my mouth more and more until the leak became a river of platitudes.

I am not a young man anymore. I know because I have heard myself starting to say these things. In my forties, I've aged light-years.

Even before my sister died, ours was not a happy family. When the local men came on horseback in February, chanting, *Donnez-moi quelque chose pour le Mardi Gras!* my brothers, Jules and John and Leon, and my sisters, Alice and Adele, would join me on the front porch with Mama to see the festivities. Daddy would come outside, too, wearing an expressionless face. Even he, the a-socialite, couldn't avoid the duties to this community. He told Alice to go around back and get Maybelline, my favorite hen, and when Alice came back from around the side of the house she handed her to Daddy and instead of tossing her up in the air like culture intended, he set her down right there on the ground, and she, not moving an inch, not even scurrying like chickens do, when she had just started pecking at some piece of rock, he cocked his leg and kicked her, lodging her into the air. *Inside*, he huffed at us, and we all did as we were told.

I swear right before she flew Maybelline looked at me, saying goodbye (Mayb didn't succumb from that kick, but after that violence she could only hop on one leg and to Daddy she was now useless and, well—).

When we got her as a chick, all fluff and down, Mama had told me Maybelline would never be dinner as long as she had control over the situation, which we both knew was never. Daddy knew I loved Maybelline and perhaps that's why he did it, to get the love out of me, to show me that little boys weren't supposed to love so much. Boys weren't put on this earth to love certain creatures.

I text her, marijuana, melatonin, Ambien, if necessary. But please, dear, sleep. I know, but sleep.

"You comin'?" Mama threw her arm around that littlest Guillory boy, little old me sitting at the kitchen table. It was Saturday and my brothers and sisters were out, running around with the other kids who rode ATVs or bicycles or walked a mile to find one another. Daddy was Somewhere. He did his own thing on Saturdays. We knew he was at Annie's Lounge, but Mama never bothered to know more than that. He had a tough job, she said, a preacher who didn't believe the gospel, he deserved a rest after the long week.

That petite boy, petite even for eight, didn't talk back then. I didn't say much at all, and if I did, it was only when spoken to. So to Mama, I nodded. *Of course I want to go.*

In the Ford Taurus we borrowed from a church-friend of Mama's, we drove the twenty minutes into town, Tammy Wynette or Conway Twitty or BeauSoleil on the radio, her hand holding mine. Like that little boy, Mama wasn't a talker or smiler, but you could feel in her touch that she carried so much love inside her she'd burst if her lips bared, exposing that love to oxygen.

"Anne-Marie! Don't think I don't know what you're looking for. Aisle six. We moved the blonde over an aisle." Miss Dominique came down from behind the tall purple-painted counter to give my mother a hug. Everyone in Lake Charles had a story, Mama and Miss Dom included. At fourteen, Mama was married to a thirty-year-old man who enjoyed tying her up and burning cigarettes on her legs, so when she escaped she stayed in the only halfway house in town. That's where she met thirteen-year-old Dominique, raped by her father and her brother until one night she walked out of her house and down Goos until she got to a gas station where a white lady picked her up and fed her dinner and gave her a shower and called the shelter the next morning. I never heard any of this from Mama. I heard it from my sister Adele, who had found an old diary of Mama's when they were helping her move her stuff from San Antonio back to Louisiana following my father's death.

There were always secrets, unsaids in my family.

"Helping your mama with her Easter hair today, Beau?"

A nod. *Yes, of course, as always.*

Miss Dominique pressed a purple kiss to my cheek.

That diary contained multitudes of buried pains. My mother and Miss Dom had never really gotten away from bad men. The new men weren't as bad as their firsts, those abusers, but they weren't good either. The new husbands were bad in the way that many men are, incapable of loving without self-interest, a type of fluid, shifting loving that led to them seeking love elsewhere, at the bar, at church, at–. They weren't men full of love like the women, love that broke them.

We didn't have much money, but Easter was coming up in a few days and there was going to be a big picnic at the church. Daddy said Mama could spend a little to get herself made up. A preacher's wife had to be presentable. *Get long hair, like Rapunzel*, is what Mama understood I was saying when I grabbed the plastic-wrapped hair, sunny-blond like Dolly Parton. Mama then, she did smile. She took the bag and we checked out.

"Unlike your mama and me, you don't need to buy hair. You have beautiful hair all on your own," Miss Dom said, placing the hair into a bag of its own, making sure Mama felt the specialness of this special occasion.

"I'll be seeing you Sunday?" Mama said.

Miss Dom came around and wrapped her arms around Mama, holding on to her, and tears fell down both of their cheeks and they sniffled quietly, not saying a word, letting unspoken truths pass between them. Miss Dom took a kerchief out of her pocket and wiped my mother's face, holding my mother's cheeks between her hands, holding her together.

Back in our driveway, the bayou behind our house humming with cicadas, Mama sitting on a metal fold-out chair folded out on the cement, I wove Miss Parton into my quiet mother's unassuming, shoulder-length hair. I tried to weave into Mama, the way Miss Dom showed me, that Parton laugh. I tried to weave that Parton boisterousness, that bubbly, smiley, no-shame-about-them-breasts woman, into my mother's hair. I didn't know who my mother was. I couldn't tell if my father had driven the joy out of her or if it was never there at all.

When I was finished, she held the blush compact to review what I'd tried to do for her. We looked at her together in the mirror, and that woman I've never known, she put her hand on my shoulder, the sky erupting in chemical-induced pink neon behind us.

While I was admiring, Alice, dressed in one of Mama's white grandma nightgowns knotted at the knee with knee-high muck boots, emerged from our teeny tiny two-bedroom house, came up behind me, lifted me up in the air by my armpits, and swung me round and round and round and round until vision fell away and everything was wet wet heat and the hissing of the cicadas and the softness of Alice's cotton dress.

Mama shouting at Alice, Alice laughing, Alice ignoring Mama, me laughing, Alice painting my face with the blood that had erupted from the re-opened wounds on her arms, me laughing, *paint me a warrior, paint me a warrior, paint me a warrior* (Alice, the only one who could get me to talk), she painting me in herself, Alice another type of warrior, whoever said warriors can't succumb, too, that warriors can't feel hurt like normal people did, people like me who were confused about our place in the world but who were made for this world and all its pleasures, who wanted all those pleasures but weren't quite sure what to do with them, we normal, confused people, Alice knew what she wanted she just wanted to be happy, an impossible thing, an impossible thing, an impossible thing.

"Go inside and clean yourselves up," Mama said.

Through the bathroom window, I watched Mama sitting out there on that metal chair. I watched her until the pink dissipated into gray and then black, until the screen door shuttered and the house met the dark outside. I did not hear the door shutter again but it did early in the morning when even the cicadas were sleeping.

There's something haunted about Leger's sculptures of tulle and cotton, an eeriness to the empty spaces that his looming (and notably, magnificent) cream puff ships and tutu castles create. To make weighty things weightless—to construct a replica of the Titanic *out of cotton balls, to remake the White House in tulle—in other words, to strip objects of the substance of their power, makes the viewer question what she has assumed about the nature of things. The spoon is metal, but maybe we can bend it with our minds. A family seems to be happy and functional, but what hard truths loom behind the smiles on the Christmas cards? What is Leger up to? It seems he is attempting to upset capital-A America. What we have believed about ourselves isn't right at all. Leger shows us how wrong we all have been.*

She says M. once told her, *There is no niche for a miniaturist.*

"A miniaturist. He was talking about me."

"Well, Bachelard said miniature is one of the refuges of greatness, so. Fuck him."

"That must make you a Gigantist."

"Someone who makes mountains out of molehills."

"But in the best way."

"Thanks, Chlo."

Alice was in the hospital, and Mama and Daddy and all of the kids were there, too, because they were all at a church function when I called and told them that Alice had done it again and that it was bad and that they needed to come and get her, quick quick. (Why hadn't I gone to church with them? Rebelliousness was rearing its head in me, *Not today, I'd said,* which happened to be my first refusal of the family, a story but not for this story.) They swung by the house so fast the car barely stopped moving, Daddy practically running through the screen door and scooping Alice up out of the tub and wrapping her in a towel before tossing her bleeding in the backseat with the kids, who screamed with her sopping, cold body on their laps.

I wasn't given instructions on what to do with myself. I was not to turn on the TV, that much I knew, not when Daddy didn't specifically say I could. I did have a marker though that I'd stolen from school. An Icy Blue like Alice's eyes. So I picked that up, and I drew pictures of the world I knew. I drew Maybelline and Miss Dom's purple lips (in blue, though, of course) and the screen door half ajar, the way Mama left it when the nights were especially suffocating and we needed more air, we needed to breathe. I drew the backseat of the truck and the bayou brimming with blue crawfish and blue horses with blue-masked men in blue-flagged clothing. I painted the world blue. Then I looked in the mirror and with that marker I drew blue cartoon tears on my cheeks. It had been years since

I was allowed to cry and sometime at school when a little girl had started to cry when she couldn't write her cursive "S" Ms. Boudreaux had knelt down beside her and instead of saying, *Shut the fuck up, shut the fuck up* she said, *It's okay to cry, Tiffany, crying is healthy, get out that hurt and you'll feel much better.* I didn't think I could cry but maybe this was close enough, maybe. All I had to do was draw the tears. All I had to do was draw.

Chloe and I are dancing, two-stepping, shit-talking, in the Tractor Supply. We came here for garden supplies, Carhartt, dog food.

"Can we have one?" she says, gazing into the large cardboard box filled with chicks, little female Brahmas selling for $1.50 a pop. Another box replete with Rhode Island Reds, another full of Stars.

"I'm not sure now is the best time to start a chicken family," I say. "You don't even have a kitchen table."

"One day I will have chickens," she says.

"One day you will have chickens," I say. "I will help you build a coop, too, if you like."

She extends her hand and we shake to a future coop.

We model overalls, camouflage, buy Sprites and jerky at the checkout.

In the truck she cries. I turn the radio up just enough so she feels alone.

Some of us are homeless in spirit. That's just the way it will always be for those who grew up moving from place to place, those who grew up not knowing the foundation of a happily betrothed mother and father with two-point-five children and a little fluffy white dog. Just like the kids with the happy homes, though, we're still tethered to the memories of our childhoods. Even when we move, the memories follow us from place to place.

Certain visions won't unstick: the leaves pasted to Alice's legs, Lake Charles lake-mud having affixed the natural decorations to her clammy skin. The water had taken her and reincarnated her as a trout, a lonesome creature of the lake. She had spent her whole life—all sixteen years of it—punishing herself for things she never did, eating and eating her agony and then starving and cutting it away. Her fishiness just affirmed the world's cruelty. She couldn't become some soft, cuddly puppy or rare and worshipped panda bear. In that swampy, chemical-saturated lake, she was doomed to swim in circles, forever forlorn.

A wealthy family found her kayak a few days later. The boat had drifted to another edge of the lake and deposited itself beneath the private dock of some oil-man. Apparently, that mother never recovered from finding our dead sister, with her arms carved up like some stigmata she had only heard about in Mass. One of the ropes with which she had tied herself to the kayak still trailed from one of the carrying handles. She wanted us to find her, knowing we'd take some small comfort in being able to put her to rest.

No one knew how she had gotten the boat out there. My family didn't own a kayak. We asked friends if they had given her the boat or if they'd helped her load it into the bed of their truck, had helped her get out there, maybe just for an evening excursion, but no one knew anything.

Alice, it was always going to be Alice. The front row just nodded through Father Broussard's eulogy.

We, people who'd lived in the same part of the swamp for one hundred and fifty years, moved to Texas, where Daddy found another job in oil refining. Louisiana was too much for us. We couldn't stand the swamps, the bays and bayous, the water that constantly taunted us, *You are not in control, give up, give up.* From then on we all feared the water. We knew it could suck us right up, turn us back into fish.

In college no one knew I was a Louisiana boy. Texas confused my accent. When people asked me where I was from, I told them I never had a place that felt like home. I avoided the question. Now, when people ask, thinking my accent some peculiar scholarly affectation, I say home wasn't something meant for me.

It's not an issue of geography. I've lived in Virginia for nearly twenty years now. But it's not home. I can't explain to you what that means. People associate home with comfort, a place to set down one's haunches, where one can make love and argue in privacy. Rest. Calm. Those things are unknown to me. I couldn't rest if I tried.

I was told boys weren't meant to love certain creatures. But I also said I was getting rebellious. When people say that about children, when they use that word *rebel* like it's the equivalent of taking the Lord's name in vain, like it's uttering the name of the Antichrist, what they mean is that the young ones are learning to be people apart from their parents. What I mean to say is that as Alice became a fish, I was getting to be myself. I was opening my mouth and the love couldn't help but come out.

Two boys stand outside a gas station off of I-10, on the outskirts of Lake Charles, Louisiana. In the wet, heavy summer night, the cigarette smoke conjured in anticipation alit by a lone streetlamp, they discover a new kind of love in the other's mouth.

As soon as it's discovered, it's gone. Tongues retreat, beads of sweat on their necks and in their armpits continue to bead, to multiply. The crosses pressed to the other's Adam's apple settle back against their owner's shivering chest.

The boys, as boys do, moved on. They created their own lives apart from one another, but, as boys do, they never did forget, they never grew up entirely.

Master Bedroom

"You've been sleeping on the floor this whole time?" Beau looks at the futon mattress, which I have been sleeping on since I moved into the house three months ago, surrounded by a sea of wood.

Up to this point, we have avoided going into this room together. No one has seen this room. Considerate, understanding, he's never asked why I keep the door shut.

"I understand." He doesn't touch me, though he feels my body vibrating next to his within the doorframe. "But it's really about time that you stop sleeping on the floor."

I am suddenly repulsed. The futon is a gray Band-Aid left on the edge of the pool.

There are many types of beds. They are much more than an arrangement of various wooden beams designed to support a mattress, where two people—or three or four—sleep, read, fuck, dream. There are marriage beds, but then there are marriage beds that also double as beds for lovers. There are race car beds designed for boys in Pull-Ups and beds with frilly, itchy pink comforters designed for girls (but Mom knows that Denise wants the race car bed and so she buys it for her, target marketing be damned). There are beds for giving birth in and there are beds for dying in.

A bed can be a very unholy cradle.

"Le Corbusier was a Fascist," M. said, when Pat and I were still a we, in the bed he shared with his wife.

"I know nothing about him. As I said, it's Beau's work."

"Is it la Villa Savoye? Reconstructed in paperclips? That makes sense." He sat up, taking the sports drink from the bedside table.

I could never imagine him running. It is nearly impossible to imagine some people in motion, sweating and huffing in neon athletic shoes on a paved suburban road.

"I just had coffee with my friend who's a fellow at the Centre Le Corbusier." He passed me the green-yellow drink. "Not that that's related in any way."

Outside the bedroom window stretched a large backyard, the vast green expanse like one you'd see in TV advertisements for ritzy lawn care services, with children hula-hooping or kicking a soccer ball, a mother throwing a Frisbee for a shepherd or retriever dog with a finely combed coat. Yet, while similar in dimension to these yards of domestic fantasy, M.'s yard was empty, overgrown, the wooden beams of the fence at the rear of the property falling into the earth. Instead of housing these domestic symbols, the grass spread its legs and shouted: *I will remain untamed, empty.*

"I'm getting up," I narrated, "to flip the record." Nude, I stood in front of the living room's bay window. Down the block, houses adorned with Christmas lights illuminated the dark street. My own home, some three hundred miles away, was also decorated, the lights on the roof hung by my husband, who was waiting for me in our bed to return from a visit to an old friend.

"This house, it doesn't feel like you. Not like the old apartment," I said, getting back into his bed.

"You're right. That apartment was perfect."

"This house was built for a family."

"This is true," he said. "I constantly feel like I've broken into someone else's house. Robbing the cradle."

"Who are your neighbors?"

"Mostly people with children."

"Is there anywhere in this town where people without children live?"

"I haven't found it yet."

He pulled the sheets up over our shoulders. Over the bed, a fleece blanket with our university's logo lay atop a cheap down-and-feather duvet. A young professor with student debt couldn't afford expensive things, though he had never been one for expensive or ornate things. His old apartment, the one I knew when we were students together, featured crooked bookshelves, books stacked on the floor against the wall, books on the coffee table, a bed pushed up against the window, which he would open in the winter, the radiator warming the sheets under which our bodies were carefully tucked, our noses grazing the cold air. We didn't mind.

Under his cheap marriage sheets, we clung to one another, to an idea compelling because of its sheer alienness to our normal lives and routines. He and I, peanut butter and kamacite. We would never be together.

"Will this ever happen for us?"

"Falling asleep?" he asked. "I do believe we will fall asleep at some point."

"You know how I feel about you," I said, searching for his eyes in the dark.

"Yes. And I feel the same way, as I told you yesterday."

In the middle of the night, I had to push him off of me. I rolled to the side of the bed where he told me to sleep. I could smell the traces of her shampoo on the pillow, something lightly coconut-y, something expensive and natural, as well as the shavings of her dry skin on the sheets. But I couldn't smell their intimacy and that was a comfort. He was mine in a way that he wasn't hers. We were each other's in a way that was not real but not unreal either.

That was the first and last time we slept together. I would go back to my home, to my marriage. I would finally figure out how to be a good wife.

I sleep with my phone by my ear. People say that you shouldn't do that, that as you slumber, electromagnetic waves will radiate out from the device and give you brain cancer.

But, I think, what if Pat calls, and the phone is on the other side of the room, on the dresser or plugged into the outlet in the bathroom, and he is vomiting or writhing in our, his, bed? I wouldn't forgive myself. I will risk the potentiality of my own cancer.

Unlike M., I chose work that could give me a different life, a life of linen sheets and goose down. From a young age I had an instinct for fine things, always managing to stop at the cashmere on the rack of sweaters. My materialism can't be helped.

I'd try to train myself out of it for the right reason. I'd give up this house and all of its furniture to be with him. Not him. What M. and I have cannot coexist alongside co-signed leases, shared utility bills, arguments over dirty dishes. We've never had anything of substance and we never will.

Some days I think Pat has no chance and some days I think he will be healthy again. But either way I have fear that I will still end up without him. I'm still hoping that my marriage can become intact again.

"The problem of your house has not yet been stated."

"What are you talking about?" I whisper into the phone, as if there's someone in the adjoining room whom I don't want to expose to our conversation. Though I am completely alone in the house. There is no one to overhear.

"You don't think your mother knows anything," she says. "But I've been around."

"Who said that I thought you knew nothing?" I say. "I know you know nearly everything."

"What problem is your house solving?"

"When did you say you are coming to visit? I need to know so I can make sure the guest room is finished by the time you get here."

"The end of December," she says. "I told you that. Are you hearing what I'm asking?"

"Christmas? I'm hearing what you're saying."

"Christmas if you like. What I'm saying is that you'll never make a house you're happy with until you know what its function is to you."

"I've never heard you talk like this."

"That's because you never listen," she says. "I've always talked this way."

"I'm not sure that's true."

"Think about what I said."

"What kind of pillows do you like? Firm, medium, or soft?"

"You know what I like."

"Firm, then," I say.

"Do you remember when you'd sleep at the end of my bed?"

"I remember I was far too old to be doing that."

"I think you did that up until you were ten years old. You wouldn't go to bed in your own room."

"I don't know what that was about. I don't know where the fear was coming from."

"Come on. You know."

"I know now. I didn't then."

"You knew what we had was special."

"You were all I had."

"Remember the firm pillows," my mother reminds me. "I can't sleep with that soft shit."

I am committed to absolutely no Christmas decorations this year. And certainly not in the bedroom. Nothing could be less erotic than Santa. Though, maybe a Santa with a big white beard and crimson cheeks on the bureau could calm my body, could distract it from what it wants. At this point, I'm not writing anything off.

Yes, Tito, you can sleep with me. Pat would not have approved, as you well know. But you are fine now. Crawl here under the sheets. Curl your body up against mine. The rules have changed.

Over email, a college classmate who now lives in the Deep South, suffering the loss of a girlfriend (to California), his job (to the economy), and his recently adopted puppy (to a tractor trailer), writes that in the Deep South, bad things tend to take place in August. The heat, the crime, the apathy, the heartbreak.

Funny, I reply. Here in the North, in the northern South, it's the other way around. Up North, bad things always seem to happen around Christmas, New Year's.

On a trip Pat and I took to Paris, the first thing I noticed was the staring. Mostly men. You'd pass by on the street and they'd look you dead in the eye, longer than a second, long enough to make you uncomfortable. I couldn't get them to take their eyes off of me. This behavior unsettled me. This happens in New York, too, I realized. How strange that in an overcrowded place, people do not have the courtesy to avert their eyes and give you your one-by-one foot of space.

Now, I'd take their eyes, any eyes. How things change.

"Good morning, Reno," the police officer says cheerfully over the radio, the sun a white shadow on his horizon. When he speaks, the phone glows a blue aureole on the pillow, a UFO's reminder. *We are not alone.*

Guest Bathroom

"Is it a window or an interpretable transparency?" Beau looks at the edges of the window in the shower, a rectangular transom painted shut.

"Why would someone do that?" I say. "There's nothing better than a window in a shower."

"An outdoor shower may be better."

"Well, in this climate, that wouldn't be practical. Maybe when we move to Key West that will make sense."

He places the head of the screwdriver at the seam of the window and hits its rubber handle with a wood-armed hammer. He works his way around the perimeter of the window, hammering and hammering. "But when we buy the pink house in Key West the priority is to enclose the existing, interior bathroom in glass, so I can look out over the sea when I shit."

"We've talked about this," I say. "I can't understand why you would want someone to see you shitting."

"If someone makes the effort to sail out there, notice me, drop anchor, and watch me in my business, then kudos to them. They've earned the show."

"Do you think Key West will happen for us?"

"It could." He pauses to blink. He rubs his eyelids, squishing and stretching them apart. I pray that a splinter from the window hasn't snuck beneath his fingernail. "But maybe it's better that we don't ever move to Key West. That we always have this fantasy ocean house."

"But what about shitting while the sea blows in over you? Don't you want that?"

He hammers once more and something pops. The paint seal has cracked. He rotates the window's plastic handle until the bottom of the window has floated six inches away from the sill. Cold air rushes in immediately.

"This is good, great," he says, sticking his fingers through the opening and wiggling them.

"Careful," I say. "A bird may think those are fat worms."

He pulls his fingers back inside and steps out of the shower. He takes me by the shoulders and I feel his tongue against my molars. This is not the first time he has tried to find love in my mouth.

"It's a shame," he says, removing his mouth from mine and folding his arms around my waist. He rests his head on my shoulder. We sway.

In our pink house, I say, people will not know what to make of us.

"That's part of the fun, isn't it?" He turns the shower's handle, initiating a trail of sputtering water down the drain. Shortly, it soothes into a stream.

I make a pot of tea. I sit on the toilet and he showers. We talk about the pink house. This is love, too.

"Do you need me to bring you anything from the house?" my mother asks.

Over the line, I can hear my mother smoking out in the yard. She never smoked until retirement. She doesn't really smoke now, but she is trying to smoke. She is trying to have a bad habit but it just cannot seem to stick.

"Nothing I can think of."

"Do you need linens?" She quiets to inhale, exhale. "Should I bring a towel?"

"No. Your bed is already made up. I have towels. We're ready for you."

"You and the dog?"

"Yes," I say.

"I'll bring linens, just in case. And tea. The kind you like."

"I have those things, but that's fine."

"See you tomorrow. And the dog."

In the early morning, too early for jogging or downward dogs or phone conversation, I wake and walk to the guest bathroom. The light in the bathroom is on and the door open, which I like to close. I dislike coming upon empty rooms. But the light is on and the door is open. This happens the next night, and then the next.

On the fourth night, I set a timer to shut the light and the door. I brush my teeth and wash my face and stare into the mirror at myself, willing to remember to shut the light, to shut the door.

On a particular Norwegian island, the lives of married women are divided into "home time" and "away time." Which is which depends on when their husbands are at sea working on oil rigs, or not. These women must make time transition smoothly between these two periods, so that the children aren't always crying for Daddy, so that routine isn't jettisoned entirely.

The Norwegian island woman's life is one of waiting. Waiting for him to arrive, but also, more poignantly, waiting for him to leave, so she can have her space, her own routines back. She spends days in anticipation of him leaving, of his returning to the rig. She yearns, as it is said, to *close the room*.

After the fourth night, I do not wake up and walk to the bathroom. I sleep through dawn. A few days pass before I try to recall whether or not the light was on when I awoke the next morning. By then, it is too late to remember. I have to move on, not knowing.

Garage

Shortly after graduating from our university, M. wrote a series of poems about a particular dumpster that sat on the edge of the campus parking lot, a dumpster that had inspired him because of its *disregarded utility*. In one poem, he placed the image of a gas cap, which, he said, was inspired by my own car's gas cap that was stuck as I had attempted to drive away from the town where we had fallen in love. Neither of us could get it off. We were trying to say goodbye. But the gas cap wouldn't budge.

At the gas pump, he wasn't listening to me as I told him about a dream I had of burning down my house, a fantasy of mine that I had lived at that point only inside of a poem.

M. has started writing about dumpsters again. This time, he is fixated on a dumpster on the campus where he now teaches. I, too, have been writing about this dumpster, which I've known only through his poetry. In the past two months, we must have exchanged nearly twenty poems about this dumpster.

I feel it, our yearning awaking from its hibernation. I want to drive four hundred miles to go and drink of him.

One day, I ask, over email, could he show me photos of the dumpster?

He sends me a link to a folder of images. The dumpster under a cloudy, steel-gray winter sky. The dumpster in early spring, buds blooming white on the dogwoods behind the parking lot. The dumpster occupied, a white mattress with yellow stains angled in its basin.

W O N D E R F U L, I write back.

A two-car garage for a one-person household.

Alternate uses for a garage, according to DIYRemodel.com:

1. Home gym
2. Home theater
3. Extra bedroom
4. Teen hang-out
5. Craft room
6. Home office
7. Yoga studio
8. Casino/bar
9. Man cave

In the latest poem M. sent, I could not find the dumpster. All the others had featured some direct reference to that yellow hulking void. But not this one.

I look at this latest email with the latest dumpster poem, sitting atop missives of condolences re: my marriage and electric bills and subscription notices to newsletters and sales sales sales. With the PDF of the poem, he attached no illuminating note. Just the attachment. He thought he was being clear.

I think I finally register what he is saying. I have found the dumpster, beating inside my own chest. *Disregarded utility.*

Pat and I kept our garage empty, so you could put what you are supposed to put in it. I even mopped once a week, because I'm that kind of person. You could perform a circumcision on the concrete. It was that bare and clean.

My mother, accruing a lifetime of things, had to resort to the garage for storage: boxes of coats and sweaters in the summer, boxes of linen dresses in the winter, boxes of unwanted clothes for Goodwill, side tables that had been replaced by side tables found at sandy antique malls by the sea. For one woman, she had so much stuff. There was no room for a car in my childhood garage.

Pat and I never spent much time in the garage. Cut into the wall was even a window that faced west. We could have had wine on a little table in there and watched the sun set.

These are the types of things you think about after it's too late.

For fifteen years, M. has offered me hope in the form of compliments, though they are also daggers. *Brilliant. Beautiful.* I know you are, but what am I?

His words glisten right before entry, enchanting, and then

they draw blood. Knives do not have to clean up their mess. Their sole responsibility is to incise. *Brilliant . . .*

W O N D E R F U L, Valerie wrote on Thomas's draft of "The Waste Land."

Those capital letters imprinted down the length of the page say more about the human condition than anything Pound wrote in the margins, or maybe even anything her husband wrote in that poem.

Brilliant. Wonderful. Beautiful.

Something I have learned as an adult: The You is always changing, but the I remains the same.

Parked in the driveway, I keep the car running. On the radio, the announcer explains how people around the world are mourning the loss of a beloved rock star. Other musicians, normal people, talk about how this stranger has changed their lives. He was seventy-six years old.

Pat is thirty-six.

I shut the engine. I cry for the rock star.

"It's just right," my mother says, stepping out of her car inside my garage. This new garage is bare, too, though not as clean as Pat's and mine. I would not advise performing surgery in here.

"You haven't even seen the inside yet."

"I have a feeling."

I gather her bag from the passenger seat, which measures the size of a diaper bag. She has just started becoming economical. It is her new modus operandi. *Never more than necessary.* She has even cleaned out the garage.

"I thought you were staying a week."

"I am. I didn't think I needed to pack a ball gown. Can we go inside?"

I go inside, into the kitchen. As much as she is beginning to contain her life, to cut back, to *downsize*, she will always be a messy human. Just not here, in my house. Even though she can't seem to keep her shoes from scattering about her own home, her purses and coats draped on dining room chairs and couch cushions, when she comes to visit, she always makes sure to bring her shoes and jacket to her room, to close the kitchen cupboards. I need to start telling her that I believe she is a good person.

But she is still standing in the garage, the door open between us.

"I want you to know I'm happy you're here," I say.

"This country is falling apart. Haven't you been watching the news? Though maybe it's no worse than it's always been."

"Yes. But what does that have to do with you being here?"

"Did I ever tell you, when I was young, my mother gave me a black baby doll?"

"No," I say.

"If it all does go to hell, I may have to live in your garage. You may have to put a little heater in there and a bed for me. I would only need a little couch and a coffee table for my books and coffee."

"You would never give up that house."

"Do you want to be a part of this world? More and more I don't. I would give up that house."

"We can talk about it, when the country dissolves."

"Give me the tour. Then can we nap?"

She enters my home through the kitchen.

Taller than my mother by a good four inches, I press her head into my neck. *You are good,* my arms around her shoulders say. *You took care of me, you take care of me. You are good. You are good.*

I write M. an email with my final dumpster poem. (This one comes without line breaks, breathless.)

> Threatening freedom, the husband goes on a walk alone to the garbage can at the end of the driveway. The family receptacle cannot contain the odor, the plastic signifier of decay, so he continues walking, on and on into the festering July heat. Confusion, as to whether or not the odor is his own, the taste in his nostrils conjuring an Egyptian garbage city, a place far from here.
>
> At the university dumpster, the one into which he has tossed many a student paper on many a world conqueror, he tosses the bag. She is not there behind him, but if she were she would tell him to quit thinking about why he is leaving. What's done is done. The details don't matter. Larry, she would say, in this wide world, there is no niche for a miniaturist.

No niche for a miniaturist, a line that now lives at the end of the final poem in a series of our poems about a dumpster. The words being the thing that will outlast us. With the poem, we roll a boulder over the cave's entrance. The end.

Backyard

More and more homeowners are fencing themselves in. A Boston fence maker estimated that his sales have risen at the rate of 45 percent per year. A Denver fence maker described his business as "golden." In Houston's yellow pages, no fewer than forty-seven fence companies advertise their wares, from waist-high chain links to six-foot cedars.

At a yard sale, I was sorting through a stack of old magazines when I came across this paragraph from a 1967 issue of *Newsweek*. We have learned that it is okay to be afraid of one another. Our neighbors, our sisters, our lovers are coming in from the street, reaching our front doors. We can practically hear their nails scratching the wood. We build walls on our lawns to keep them out.

We are constantly surrounding ourselves with fences.

Just because you can't see them doesn't mean they aren't there.

Chain links, please keep Daddy away.

A shed sits at the edge of my property, where my land meets my neighbor's. The shed is tucked beneath a large oak tree. It is a mess, to put it lightly. Holes pockmark the concrete floor, through which strands of grass stick up their necks. Formations of dirt follow from the door, which sits askew on its hinges and requires lifting off of its resting place on the ground to open or shut. Pieces of cardboard sit on the rafters, someone's half-effort to block out the rain.

The shed is empty. No garden tools or washing machine or hobby desk where somebody glued pre-cut balsa wood together to make a ship or a plane. Just a space that someone had cut out beneath the trees, maybe just to prove that they could.

I am trying to take it back from nature. Apologies. I have plans for this space.

I am inspecting one of the shed's three windows. Water has seeped in and the stool has begun to rot. With a hammer I pry it out. The wood is thick and particular, and except for the rotted wood, there are no signs of frass. No termites have penetrated this wood. Cypress. Someone built a cypress shed here, though there is not a cypress tree for hundreds of miles, perhaps out of longing for their original home.

At the showing, my Realtor assured me that it could easily be torn down.

I could never. This is memorial architecture. This was

someone's temple. Is. It would be criminal to tear it down. I
can't. I have plans for this place.

We are supposed to be shopping for furniture, but instead
my mom and I have stopped for pedicures in a salon decorated with plastic horse figurines. We are staring at a large
glass tank with a large gray-brown fish who can barely turn
around in his tank, and we are feeling sorry for the fish.

"His name is Conrad," Phillip, our nail technician, says.
Phillip wears fifty-five years light around his shoulders; he is
thin and angley. He has already left us once to take a smoke
break. He tells us he loves the countryside. He used to live in
New York City, but all he did was work, work, work and at the
end of the day he would go to a bar. He says he can go to a
bar anywhere. Why should someone have to work more just
to do the same thing? *You understand me*, he says to my mom
and me.

My mother and I share the same feet. Our calluses are thick
and break into crusty, desert plateaus. We joke that perhaps our
calluses are the reason we have trouble retaining men.

Mom is looking at her hands.

"Did you want a manicure, too?" I ask.

"These hands are the reason you're here, you know."

"As a surgeon, that makes sense. The hands pay the bills."

"Yes, but that's not what I was referring to."

Inside the salon, there is no ventilation. When we first
walked in, we worried about the chemicals, but we sat down
anyway.

"When I was in the orphanage—I don't think I ever told

you this—your grandfather and grandmother were just walking through. As he was passing by, I reached out and grabbed him. He looked at me, picked me up, and that was it. If I hadn't done that, we wouldn't be sitting here. We would not be getting high on chemicals in a nail salon in Virginia."

In the tank, Conrad floats like a submarine, his weight making his movements incremental, heavy. He looks miserable.

"He gets angry if I don't talk to him," Phillip says, taking my mother's hand. "Manicure? Yes. Manicure." He continues, "I've had Conrad fifteen years. If I feed him too much, he will die. I can never feed him too much. He's my boy." Phillip sets my mother's hand down on the spa chair's armrest and walks closer to the tank. He clicks his tongue and taps his finger on the glass. *Come, Conrad. Come.* Glacially, Conrad swings his body around to face Phillip. His small fins flap with great effort, bringing his body closer and closer to his father until their noses are touching.

"I've never seen anything like that," we agree.

"Is it just you two?" Phillip says, returning to my mother's feet.

Just us.

"No husbands? No kids?" he says.

My mother points at me. "She's it."

"And you? Where is your baby?"

I pull out my phone and show him photos of Tito. Playful Tito on his back in a patch of light on the wood floor. Tranquil Tito in my bed, nose tucked between his paws. *My boy.*

"No human boy?" Phillip asks.

We look at our feet, our hard edges polished off, the nails buffed and painted red (Mom) and nude (me). We have a couple weeks of smoothness before the desert reclaims our soles. We look at our hands, how much daintier they are, beautiful even. Thin fingered, elegant, good for enticing, lovemaking, caring, rearing.

"I made it," I say to my mother. We hover over the kitchen island, looking down at a surprisingly perfect (to both of us) pie.

"Really? I didn't know you baked. Is this something you're doing now?"

"I thought I could learn finally, at the tender age of thirty-four."

Above our heads, the single bulb of the ceiling lamp illuminates the bulbous red of the pie's cherries. Encapsulated by light, we cannot make out the shapes of trees outside. The yard reads black. If someone were to peer in at us, a someone we couldn't see through the dark, they would think we looked like actors on a movie set. We look staged, play-acting domesticity. My mother eats the pie, dutifully and with a glimmer of pleasure.

"Is it good at all? This is a new recipe."

"Aren't they all new? And yes. It's perfect."

"This is what we are supposed to do after dinner in this house, right?" I say.

"What are you saying? I said the pie was great."

"I don't know if I'm doing any of this right."

Her hands are on my face. Her fingers are sticky on my cheeks. She rubs her thumbs away from my nose, mixing the

red juice with my dew, repeating this motion like she's painting my face. Her thumbs sing, *It's right. It's right. It's right.*

Some women do this all their lives. Iron, rear, sweep, wash,
fold, brush, wipe. For the entirety of their adult lives, they
make homes. They make other people. They make families.

This is just to say that what I'm doing is not so unusual.
It's the opposite. This act is completely mundane.

But no one talks about how difficult it is. I don't think it's
any easier for a woman with a pretty husband and a pretty
six-year-old daughter. Beneath the prettiness, we are all a
mess. We are all struggling. We do not know how to make a
home.

Let's leave bleach stains on the darks together. Let's put
too much sugar in the cake and celebrate our efforts, our fail-
ures. Let's commemorate the spoiled milk, the missed school
bus, the unwashed faces at bedtime, the unmown yard.

In the beginning, Pat and I would drive around looking at
houses. We would park our car down the street, so as not to
draw attention, watching for oncoming traffic as he grabbed
my hand and led the way along the side of the road up to the facade of the house. We would take photos of these houses, many
of which were not for sale at all. Not that it mattered—we were
not in the market for a house. We barely knew one another. Unlike other young couples, we didn't go to the movies, cradling a
mutual silence in dark theaters between our fingers. We would
look at houses, standing at the edges of their yards, of the lives
inside, and imagine if we would have something as beautiful.

Driving around the countryside, we discovered a particularly dreamy home, a shed house hidden behind a patch
of pine. The house was all colliding geometry, modern in its
willingness to jut out in uncompromising angles, but also traditional in the way its simple wood exterior harkened back to
the farmhouses and barns that once populated this region. We
fell in mutual love.

That house . . . he sighed via text, his digital breath attest-
ing to our harmony, our shared vision.

In less than two years, not that house, but a different
(rental) house, would be ours.

Cybil

Pat's oncologist says, *About a week*. That's how long someone can go without food and water, but that's pushing it, really.

"Why are you asking this?" Dr. Varma, Raj, says. "You're not going to drag yourself into the woods and die, are you, Pat?"

Raj could have been a stand-up comedian, but instead he chose to tell people they were dying, in two months, two years, a situation that offers its own form of humor, I suppose. As an oncologist, you have a captivated audience, which is half of the challenge.

Pat tells him that is not his plan. It's just a question.

Like, how many licks does it take to get to the center of a Tootsie Pop?

Like, what is the square root of three hundred and ninety-six?

Like, Doctor, what does the cancer look like? Under a microscope, does it look like an algae bloom? Does it look like rainfall on wet asphalt? Like a concerto of the skin? (Neither his questions nor mine, just questions.)

We sit silently in Raj's office, the walls covered with photos in mismatched frames of his children; his grandchildren; his wife, Neha, who in her teen years was some kind of model back in Bangalore. I would see her at hospital parties draped in chiffon of a bright hue. By his side, her elbow rested lightly on Raj's shoulder, hip propped and displayed as only perpetually thin women can get away with.

"So you will be going with him to these chemo appointments," Raj says.

Of course, I say.

We are sparing her this.

We are sparing her the phlebotomist and the tile floors and the hospital gowns and the patchy beard and the vomiting.

We are sharing her house while she sits alone in a different, un-worn-in house, just twenty minutes down the road.

We are doing this for her.

"You are a good mother-in-law," Raj says.

I am not quite that anymore but I am still a mother. I am doing this for her.

"It's so quiet in this house," I say to Pat in the foyer. I do not say, *Without my daughter.* "And there's no dog hair anywhere. I suppose you must be enjoying that. Though I've ruined that with Henri."

"He's welcome here, I've told you," he says. "I need to lie down." We are barely inside the house and he is walking up the stairs, to their bedroom.

"You are not feeling lonely, are you?" I ask, but he is already up the stairs, ready to forget the afternoon, to exchange the faux leather chair and IV for plush pillows and a down comforter.

On his bedside table, I set down two gallons of water and two thirty-two-ounce Gatorades. "In a few hours, I'll come and check on you."

The stairs creak. This house is full of old wood and heart-warming details. Good bones, as they say. On finding this house, Chloe said *Oh* and *Ah* at every ceiling medallion, every art deco–era tile, every touch of ornamental plaster, the slide of the pocket doors between the foyer and the living room. She is not easily impressed, so this meant that this house was particularly special, that she had high hopes for this house.

It is not yet four o'clock. I cannot call Chloe and say, *Hi, dear, would you like to grab coffee? I just happen to be in town* . . . It's easiest not to complicate things, to make her wonder.

The insides of his kitchen cabinets are empty as lungs. There is coffee in the freezer and a bag of pistachios in the cupboard by the fridge with the glasses, not even in the cabinet where the food should be. He would probably feel the emptiness of his new life more intensely if he put the one lonely bag of pistachios in the food cabinet. Sometimes all it takes is one small thing, a bag of pistachios, to reveal what you now lack.

I cannot leave the house. If I wander off to the grocery store, I risk the chance of running into her. Maybe her store ran out of the bread she likes and she had to run to the one over here. It is a nicer grocery store. Everything is nicer over here.

I am afraid I can't help him get better. I am afraid that she will learn to know love as abandonment. I have never wanted her to be like me.

The French word for caretaker, concierge, means *fellow slave*. Equals. He and I are shackled to the same suffering.

"Alone? How can you leave her like that?" Her father is on the phone, reprimanding me.

"She is not alone. Her friend Beau stays over there every few nights. I talk to her every day."

He has called to check on Chloe, but he will not call her directly. He is assessing the situation from afar, determining, through my commentary, when it is best for him to swoop in and be Dear Daddy. It is a familiar act.

"So are you calling her or what?"

In the drive Pat is waiting for me. My car is running and the exhaust is shooting out hot into the sub-freezing air. Through the window of his house and the driver's window I can see his head tilted back at an angle of rest. He is not even halfway through his treatments and he is always tired, he is always sleeping. In some ways it is like having a newborn again. As a baby Chloe could practically sleep on command. Reclining on the couch, needing rest after a few nights on call, I'd lie her on top of me and she'd nod off against my chest, sleeping until I stirred. We harmonized in a way I didn't think possible for two people.

"I will," Daniel says.

"Soon?"

"When I feel like it, Cybil."

We hang up the phone.

When we first met, he wore a mustache and light-wash jeans. He had sort of a George Michael look without the jewelry but with all the great hair, chest, head. He was proud of his butt, probably still is. The mustache, and the tight jeans, for that matter, were the style then, and I suppose they are the style now. That's how things work. There is no new way to part one's hair.

He was always holding me to him in public, pulling me closer. I wanted him to be the father of the children I never knew I wanted.

In the pre-marriage days, we would walk from car to grocery hand in hand, my belly flat still, his jacket on my shoulders against the heatless desert night. Then, we worshipped at the altar of Potential.

There is no new way to part one's hair, no new type of love. There is no husband and children, but there is Chloe. There is no new love, there is Chloe.

I thread my gloves onto my fingers and get into the car.

"Are you ready?" I ask, placing my hand on Pat's forehead. His skin is cool enough.

"Can't wait."

I buckle my seatbelt, thinking of all of them.

We did not celebrate Valentine's Day. Neil was never the kind of man for that, and I was not the kind of woman for that, at that point in my life. But I had a brief, necessary break from my rotations and needed to get out into the heat and sun and move. Those days I was always under hospital lighting, the

cold blue-white corridors my only walks, the luminescent ger-
bera daisies in vases and seascapes cheaply framed my only
scenery. The day before we had decided to hike Ventana Can-
yon. We wanted to see the Window, an opening in a craggy
formation of rock in the Santa Catalina Mountains. The night
before we'd packed water and suntan lotion into backpacks
and laid out caps and hiking shorts and hiking socks and hiking boots so we could leave early, without too much fuss. We
planned to get out before the heat became too much.

"Are you ready?" he asked, finding me on the patio.

I stood on the slab of concrete that jutted out from the
front-left side of our rented ranch house in my sports bra and
shorts, barefooted. "Look," I said.

By the garage, a red, Chihuahua-sized combination of
snout and hoof and fuzz scurried in circles. Red screeched a
terrible screech. Nowhere in sight followed its javelina mother.
Red was lost and alone and we could hear that.

"We need to go," he said. "It is getting late."

I slipped on sandals that had been bleached from sienna
to wheat by the sun and went back into the house through the
sliding glass doors, through our bedroom, a cave of unmade
sheets (no hospital corners here) and a bureau top dusty with
granola bar crumbs and lack of attention, out through the
living room and shaded entranceway enclosed by a wrought-
iron door, out into the morning air that was dense with dust
and earth and smells like something primordial.

I knelt down, within feet of Red, here kitty-kittying.

Screech screech, the creature said, louder suddenly, maybe
with relief. I must have smelled like Mama in my morning
muskiness, sweat accrued in sleep, because Red came up to

me, grazing my ankles, nestling in the space between my knees. I took the towel and picked Red up in it.

"I'd still like to go," he said, coming up behind me.

"He needs to go to a refuge." Red was peeping now, soft peeps. "Maybe the desert museum will take him."

"We've been wanting to do this hike," he said.

"What would you like me to do? Leave him here?"

"He lives in this desert. He knows what to do here without you."

Maybe Red began screeching again, more loudly, more urgently, or maybe that was just my imagination.

Red's pink nose grazed my lips and I did not wipe away his wild smell. I was still standing in the drive when Neil went back into the house, picked up his backpack, returned to the drive, to our station wagon, got in, put a hand out the window, and waved goodbye. We were standing there, Red and I. He thought I was his mother and for a number of moments I did not tell him otherwise.

"I have to have you know, at least, why I'm doing this," Pat says, his head pillowed on the couch, his body horizontaled by exhaustion. "You have to know that I think this is how it has to happen."

Across from him, I am all put together, neat and presentable in red slacks and a heavy red cardigan with gold enamel buttons. He looks like shit. I tell him this and he laughs. He's wearing a button-down shirt, though beneath the blanket I can see he's wearing pants with an elastic waistband.

"She knows this is real," I say. "She doesn't think you are lying."

"Yes. But."

"Explain why. Yes. Explain."

He sits up, adjusts the pillows behind his lower back. I reach behind him and plump the pillows. He pats, too. We plump together.

"Whatever I say will sound like it's not enough. I'll sound like a fucking asshole no matter what."

"That's possible," I say. "Yes."

"If I say I'm doing this because she is too young to have to do this and she will likely have to do this again, at a more appropriate age, that I'm saving her the first time, you won't believe me."

"You understand that," I say, "just because you're not physically together, that just because she's not driving you to chemo and holding your hand in the chair, she's still going through this, right?"

"Or if I say, I'm doing this because I don't want her to see me fall apart in that house, our house. That it should be a hopeful place, not a place of fucked-up memories."

I do not say, *You know that, just because you aren't sick there, vomiting into that toilet late at night, her house can still become haunted by your pain?*

"You won't believe me," he says, again. He buttons the top button of his shirt, and then unbuttons it again. He unbuttons all the buttons and tosses the shirt on the couch. In a T-shirt, worn through, he looks like a little boy.

"Now you know what menopause feels like."

"You look very nice," he says. "You put me to shame."

"At this age, you can't leave a hair out of place."

I hand him the bottle of Gatorade, diluted, the other half of the liquid concoction in the fridge. In the fridge, I've assembled an army of new Gatorade bottles and old Gatorade bottles filled with the half-and-half mixture. When he drinks the dilution, we joke about pretending to be on a golf course in Miami, sipping Arnold Palmers. Neither of us has ever golfed or had any desire to, but this absurdity is part of the fantasy. Anything is better than the situation we're in.

I go to the other side of the room, to the table in the hallway where my purse has been sitting for the past three months while I've stayed in this house, tending to my daughter's husband. "Your skin is dry, isn't it? Your hands are cracking. Here."

"You keep everything in that bag. Lotion, crossword puzzles. What else?"

He lets me squeeze a large dollop into his palms. He does the work of making a fire between his hands, in between his fingers.

"Not a word to her, right, about all of this." He looks at me, telling me, as if we haven't had this same conversation a ship-full of times before.

"Trust me," I say. "Won't you?"

"You're her mother."

Meaning, *I have her best interest at heart.*

"I'm not asking for much from you," I say, "but I do have one question."

"Am I doing this right?" he asks.

"You've never applied lotion before, clearly."

"Never the right way," he says.

"Give me your hands."

He levitates his hands in front of me. I pull them to rest on my knees and knead the cream into one hand.

"After all this, after you're better," I begin to say.

"You're wondering what I will do, if I will talk to her again."

"Not talk."

"I know what you are saying. Not talk. Start over again."

I push the lotioned hand off of my knee and take the other, pressing it against my knee.

"I can't answer that."

We stare at his hands like we expect them to make the next move, to decide the future for us both. Since I've been staying here, he has avoided all talk of her. You cannot help but talk about the one you love. Her name cannot help but fall from your lips at any conversation, whether it be about Magic Erasers or marriage. With Pat, in her house, there has barely been a murmur about Chloe. I am a fool.

After moments of nothing I set the bottle of lotion on the coffee table and point to it. "You're soaked in it. Now go rest."

He goes up to bed in my daughter's once-ago dream house. I wait around awhile before sleep.

We are at a wine bar and it is happy hour, too early to be at a wine bar, but Raj likes this place. He loves wine. He and Neha traveled to Burgundy this past summer and sat around drinking for two weeks straight, or so he says. He is not a drunk, or maybe he is. Who can ever know until you are in bed and they do not come home?

"How are you?"

"As fine as one can be," I say. We are outside on the small, roped-in patio, which is part of a larger bricked thoroughfare full of shops and small restaurants. It is not raining but it is cloudy and humid, like it could rain at any minute.

"You haven't told your daughter?"

"No. She doesn't need to know."

"Well, I don't know about that."

The waiter comes over with a bottle. Raj sticks his nose into the empty heart of the glass, swirls the red liquid, pours the contents of the glass into his mouth, holds the liquid in his cheeks like an old cowboy holds dip. He swallows, finally, and nods his head at the waiter.

"This seems like a bad idea," he says, filling my glass.

"That is not why I'm here, to be reprimanded."

"That is a nice jacket," he notices. "I like the buttons."

College students file into the bar. They bring with them backpacks and laughter and youth. Some of them may be Raj's students. Medical students have more time than they used to. There are stricter rules now. You can't work students three days on call in a row. Of course, that means they don't get the same experience as we did, working sleeplessly, needing to react to a crisis unprepared without the hand-holding of a supervising doctor. Things have changed, but maybe they are happier.

"So you want to know how he is doing?"

"Yes," I say, rubbing my fingers along the stem of the glass. I drink, not looking at him.

He adjusts the silk scarf around his neck, flattening and smoothing the edges against his chest. He wears expensive beiges and whites that have small, just detectable stains on the pant legs and down the fronts of his button-downs. Reclined in the cafe table chair, his ankle is crossed and residing on the knee of the other leg. A royal purple sock brightens out from under the hem of his pant leg.

"More. Please. Just a little bit," I tell him, as he tops off my glass.

"He should be fine." He crosses his arms over his chest. He is a man that is always in a position of repose, but he is not as comfortable as his posture makes him out to be. "Are you relieved?"

"That is a complicated question."

When he laughs, his body rocks forward and he presses a hand to his paunch.

"I have to tell you, you need to relax. You've known that his prognosis was positive for some time."

A young man with blond-white hair and white skin comes over to Raj and takes his hand. Raj's eyes alight, and he holds the man's, the just recently boy's, hand in his as they greet one another, make talk.

"This here is one of the best OBs you'll ever meet," he says, introducing me.

"Was." I drink to empty my glass.

"Yes," he says, turning to the man. "I will see you later, in a few hours."

The blond-white man disappears back inside the bar with his entourage.

"He's a bright one. He has a good sense of the patient." He leans into me and grabs my hand. I believe he is devoted to

Neha, but he is touchy with everyone, leaving enough room for wonder. "You will be fine. You have good instincts and you followed them. Now do not worry. How much longer will you be in town?"

"I guess not much longer now."

"Well, it has been good to have you around. We both know how hard a good friend is to come by for people like us."

"People like us?"

"Physicians. Aliens. Strangers to this place."

I squeeze his hand. He takes my hand and holds my wrist up to his nose. "J'adore?"

"Who doesn't?"

His laugh releases my hand from his. We laugh together.

"I need to get back."

"Come on!" He picks up the wine bottle, shaking the contents to show how much drinking there is left to do.

"I think you can handle it without me." I rise from my chair and he, too, rises. We meet at the middle of the table and kiss one another's cheeks.

"It will be fine! You will be fine!" he calls out after me. As I leave, there is laughter and another bottle ordered. The blond-white boy wanders back to our table, taking my place.

There were perfect moments, with both of my husbands.

While living in Wisconsin, Neil and I'd go to this particular French restaurant, whenever we could scrounge up the money to do it. The waiter knew us. Charlie. He liked us. Well, he liked Neil. After one meal—the oeuf cocotte au foie gras!—we came out and our car was dotted in croissants.

Little crescents on the windshield, on the trunk, even croissants perched on the side mirrors. At first, this made us sad.
We wanted to stuff them all in a bag and take them home
and cherish every bite. But, as we later found out, they were
trash croissants. The pastry chef had messed up the dough, so
Charlie was putting them to good use in giving them a new
life of mischief.

What else was there to do but start a little war? A torrent
of croissants flew back and forth across the car, littering the
parking lot with slivers of the moon. Driving home, we could
barely contain ourselves, our clothes slipping at the facade of
the apartment.

Or, years later, Chloe, Daniel, and I on the way home from
the hospital after she was born. Chloe and I in the backseat. It
was Orchestral Suite no. 3 in D minor playing on the radio. I
wanted a drink. He stopped at a liquor store and bought a bottle of Laphroaig, and the three of us sat in the backseat of the
liquor store parking lot, Daniel and I sipping from the bottle.

Neil left me (for a younger woman, a natural blonde with
the luxury of time and energy to contribute to doting) like all
of our loves leave us: quietly, loudly, suddenly, predictably,
with many traces, crumbs inedible.

Daniel, the Father of Chloe: He is a story I cannot yet tell
myself.

From this view, it may not seem like it, but I have loved,
root and branch.

When my life is not this strangeness, I can be found at home.
That may seem like an obvious statement, but some people al-

ways seem to be out and about, running errands, lunching and dinnering with friends and acquaintances, ellipticaling at the gym, road tripping on weekends, whereas I like to be home. There is nowhere better than the quiet of home.

The house I live in, the house I bought over thirty years ago now, is the house I chose for Chloe. This neighborhood's name has the word *lake* in it, but the body of water behind my house is really a man-made pond, a lovely pond with water and algae, nonetheless. It does not disappoint, as far as ponds go. This pond homes geese, many of them. In the winter, down they come from Canada and take the water as their temporary home. The pond is also home to an array of fish. For twenty years, a neighbor across the pond has stocked the water with bass. The geese know this, somehow. Also, snapping turtles. Once, Chloe found one up the hill from the pond in our front yard. *He looks naked. He needs a hat.* And so she placed, carefully, an Uncle Sam–style top hat, paper red white and blue, on its head. He cocked back and shot his neck at her. But she was okay. There were no accidents that day.

The call of the geese. The quiet. The road to our house curves down and away from the main street of the suburb, ending at the three-bedroom prairie house tucked in between some grass and trees.

The house itself needed work. Hardwood throughout the living and dining rooms and kitchen, but an ugly amount of carpet, it's true. Wallpaper. So much of it, the 1980s kind, *floral*. It'd strike fear in you, the wallpaper.

For Chloe and me it was just right. With its big windows and open spaces, she would always be able to find me, to know

I was there. Even now that she's grown up and gone, it's still what I need. It's me. It's just right.

"I need you," Chloe says over the phone.

"Baby," I say. "I'll come over this weekend."

"I know we said the end of December but now would be better."

"Yes."

"Would you still come around Christmas, too? I'd like to have you and Beau for dinner."

"Don't eat me," I say.

"Not what I meant, Mom."

"I'm sorry. I'm just kidding. Just trying to help."

"I will make sure I put the firmest pillows in your room."

"Whatever is fine. Whatever works."

"Mom, we both know that is not true."

"Well, I'll be there."

"I love you."

"I love you, too," I say.

Henri barks. Pat calls. *Cyb. Cyb.*

"Hold on," I say. "Just a few days."

Even though I'm retired now, people still want baby stories. People always want to hear about the deformities, the deliveries of babies conjoined, missing limbs, possessing noses without nostrils. They do not want to hear about the healthy babies, or even the syndromes that hide, the Marfan, the autism. I do not offer them more than this one story. If they want protracted horror, they can read the news.

A cyclops?

Yes. That is the actual medical term (cyclopia).

What did the mother think? Seeing the baby come out with one eye? Can you imagine, seeing a baby come out of you that had one eye? I can't. I'd die.

That's what the baby did. She didn't survive for more than a few minutes.

I don't know what I'd do. I don't know how I could carry that baby the whole nine months.

Well, you wouldn't. Now we can tell from the ultrasound. Most people choose to abort.

Oh. Well. That's a relief. I mean, for the baby. For the mother and the baby.

I give them what they want, complete the story for them, but their imaginations want to keep on running. As some people fantasize about healthy babies, others fantasize about disaster. Sometimes, those people are the same people. They never ask, *What was the delivery you are proudest of? What delivery was the most exuberant? What delivery changed your life?* No. They want cyclopia, they want heartbreak.

Neil was the love of my life. It is easy to see, to say that now. For some, love comes early in a brief bright burst. It is not meant to last long. What do they call those flowers that bloom only for a day? All radiance for twenty-four hours and then, nothing. But we still appreciate that flower, whatever its name, for offering even a passing glimpse at its beauty.

What the hell do they call it? Beau would know something so obscure. Chloe is always sending me apps I should download for sharing lists of books we both should read and identifying songs I like on the radio. Why not turn his brain into a piece of software? *Ask Beau.*

In the kitchen there is pie. My daughter's pie. Really one of the most beautiful pies I've seen. And this is her first pie.

"Is it good at all?" she asks. "This is a new recipe."

"Yes," I tell her. "It's perfect."

"Is this what we are supposed to do after dinner? Is this what's right?"

"Chloe. I said the pie was great."

"I feel like I'm failing at all of this. What do I do? What am I supposed to do?"

I want to make her feel better. I want her to know that home making is no simple task, that it requires erring and erring and tears and gin. Messing up is part of the process. These bumps and depressions are part of it. She needs to know that she doesn't need her little dog or some husband to do it. She can do it on her own. Some of us have no other choice.

My fingers taste red and sweet. The skin of her cheeks taste the sweetness, I hope, too. I hope she hears my thumbs sing, *It's alright. It's alright. It's alright.*

In the car at the McDonald's parking lot, warming ourselves over a carton of French fries, she is telling me about this dream she is having, about a shed or shack on the edge of the sea, and I ask, "What does it tell you about what you're feeling, this dream?"

"It's obvious, isn't it? I'm supposed to be comforted on this beautiful island, but I'm stranded here. I'm stuck. The water is biting at my feet. I could be overtaken by the sea at any moment."

"That's how you feel?"

"I feel like he's marooned me here."

Later that afternoon, in her shed, she is caulking windows. Her coat puffs up and around her face. Strands of her fur collar cling to her wind-chilled lips.

"It is a bit cold to be doing this, isn't it?" I say.

"It needs to be done."

She does not say, *There is no one else to do it for me.*

"You have not talked to Pat, have you?" she asks, one arm propped on her hip and the other bent vertical, the caulking gun in ready position.

Through the gaps in the doors and windows, the wind forces its way into the shed. The glue hardens against the cold air.

I tell her everything that she wants to know, nothing more. Now she knows enough, enough to hurt her, to maroon her on an even more remote island, without even her mother for comfort. But this is a mother's job, too. To teach her she needs to be able to survive on her own. To show her that when I die she will not die, too. She will go on caulking and loving and fearing.

For two days, she does not say a word to me. She does not tell me to leave, but she does not say much more than to ask me if I'd like a cup of coffee in the morning. I keep to myself while she works in the shed. During the day there is hammering and power drilling and in the night there is the sound of water filling pots and chicken roasting in the oven, the hush of doors closing. During the day there is the *shh* of sitting on the couch with a book and in the evening the dull rhythm of slicing vegetables. There is the quiet that comes from leaving doors open, of waiting for her.

"The Golden Arches never looked so golden," he says. His fingers weave in his lap. He searches out the car window for what other people have been doing while he was in a hospital room thinking about the cells mutating inside of his body. This is normal obsessive behavior for undergoing chemo. To wonder how other people go on ordering McFlurries when chaos is at work in the molecular.

"Soon enough, you can have all the Big Macs you want."

"By then I won't want them anymore," he says.

I say, "Yes. Isn't it funny how life works?"

In his driveway, the car hums, waiting for him to get out. He coughs but manages the exit by himself, brushes off the notion of French fry salt from his pants.

I assure him, "You will be fine doing this on your own."

This house looms for such a small house. Solitary on the corner and full of presence. The only one like it in the neighborhood. It is not meant for just one person, one man. I still hope that he recognizes his error, soon.

"Will you call her?" I do not need to say, *When you are better*, because we both know that he will, eventually but soon enough, be free of the disease. Which means that soon he will have to deal with normal life problems, if not with Chloe than with a new woman, tiffs over toothpaste left open on the bathroom counter, jealousy over Another Man, things that he may have thought he would never have to think about again. I wonder, does his surprise health bring lukewarm feelings?

He says, *Of course.* The front door shuts and locks after him. *Of course. Of course. Of course.*

There is no dirt in heaven, the welcome mat says. We lay it at her door.

"Ridiculous. It's just what I needed," my daughter says.

She has already outfitted my car for the road. A thermos full of coffee (black, strong) and a travel bag of snacks (cashews, leftover Halloween candy), though the drive is only two hours and change.

"I can stay longer, if that's what you need," I say.

"No. I have a lot to do. And you need time alone."

"But I'd go a little longer without that for you. You know that."

"I know."

She opens the garage door. Outside the light is hazy, the sky impeded by clouds. It could snow or rain. Around my neck she wraps a pashmina, weaving the silk around and around before tying it off. Like a good French girl she kisses me on both cheeks and then hugs me deeply, without a preference for personal space, like a good American girl.

"See you at Christmas," I say.

"Don't forget your pillow," she says.

They say that when a woman carries a child, fetal cells cross through the placenta, enter her body, course through her bloodstream, take refuge in her liver, her lungs, her thyroid, her heart, her skin, and eventually wander all the way up to her brain where they stay, indefinitely.

I wonder if every mother, the ones I create and the ones I

will never meet, have the same thought at some point in their lives, the good ones and the bad ones and the in-betweens (that area where most of us fall). I wonder if we all share the same hope, to have the same magic power somehow bestowed upon us: to travel back to one afternoon early in our child's life, a week to a few weeks after birth, when our bodies have started to heal and we are getting reacquainted with the world of routines. It is that moment when Daddy is away and all the other caretakers have left us in peace, and the baby is at your breast and you never in your life had such a feeling in your chest, this knowing that you can never let her go, that you will forever be connected in some mystical way. This moment of harmony is not the moment of conception, when she is only partially on your mind. This moment is the moment of connection between her lips and your breast, where there is no separation, physical or metaphysical. In this moment you know that for all the trauma you have suffered, for all the suffering you have witnessed, you know there is no love greater than this and you believe in God.

That fact makes so much sense. In those nine months, you feel yourself becoming her. Maybe that is why it is easy to call women crazy, bipolar, mad, split personalities. We are carrying two people inside of us at once.

The Other House

I am not expecting the color of his cheeks, engorged in pink-
ness, when he opens our, his now, front door, and when I lean
in to embrace him for the first time. I am not ready for the mus-
cles in his biceps, which stiffen as his arms wrap around me.

"You were not expecting this," Pat says, taking my coat
and waving me into the foyer.

"But that's a good thing."

He leads me to the couch. It, and a coffee table I do not
recognize, an iron-and-glass-top construction that only a
certain type of man without a woman could find appealing,
are the only pieces of furniture in what was once our family
room. On top of the glass he has set an unpressed French
press. A small stream of vapor floats out from the edges of the
lid, floating away down the hall back toward the front door.
In the winter, we had to roll up towels and shove them beneath the doorframe. Our house could get so drafty. We would

hold one another close on this couch, but the cool found its way into our bones anyway.

We sit next to one another, our knees turned inward toward one another. I scoot away so that my back is up against the arm of the couch.

"I won't stay long," I say.

"Why don't you? I'd like you to."

"I need to run to Lowe's and get more paint."

"You're still doing that?"

"Painting? Yes. Of course. Rome, you know."

"Rome?"

He scoots himself closer to the coffee table and presses the plunger of the press down, sending oaky bubbles speeding to the surface. The couch is too soft. His thighs shake as he pours me a cup, balancing on his fragile legs, which have not regained the musculature of his pre-cancer body. He is not completely put back together. Part of me sighs in relief.

"Shouldn't we talk about how you are feeling?" I ask.

"Thankfully, there is not much to discuss."

"Then what can we talk about?"

"There's you to talk about," he says.

"If it disappeared, the cancer, then where did it go?"

"That is the question." He pauses. "Do you want to see the CT scan?" He gets up from the couch and goes into another room. I cannot hear him rustling through a drawer or opening a cabinet.

He sits down, hands me the plastic image.

"That is beautiful," I say. His insides reveal a void, a black and gray openness. He is free. "May I have it?"

"Of course," he says, unsurprised.

I hold the scan and raise it above my head, like I'm going to give a rousing speech, like I'm going to tell him that now that nothing is holding us back we must be together, that *we* are free, not just him.

But like a statue I begin weeping, from my armpits, my eyes. He stands and reaches for me, this discarded Venus that he put out on the road for someone else to take. He rubs my cheeks, giving me a last polish.

Pat

There were always secrets between us. Though I'd be lying if I didn't admit that she never wanted it that way from the beginning. When we were first married, first dating, even, she wanted me to tell her everything. She wanted nothing to be off-limits. Like, if we were having a conversation, and I got distracted by some blip in my brain, my monkey mind following some new thread, she would ask, *But what are you thinking? Where did your brain go?* Or, if we were in bed, and we had been silent for a stretch of time, she would say, *But what are you thinking now?* And then, moments later, when another bridge of silence was built, *And what now?*

I would say *nothing* because at a time like that most people's brains aren't really focused, aren't in the right state for complex thinking. For the times that I was indeed thinking about something, *nothing* stood in for all the things with which that moment didn't need to bother, those stray thoughts from the recesses of the mind that slip through the fence when they're not supposed to.

Over time, she became very used to this idea of unknowing. She accepted that some things were off-limits to the other. But I wasn't deliberately trying to hide. I had nothing of consequence to keep from her.

Secrets is probably the wrong word. That makes it sound as if I were trying to keep important things from her, things that would break her heart if she discovered them. Really, what I was keeping from her were inconsequentialities, afternoon dry cleaning pick-ups and near-missed phone conferences, things like that.

I think we were both okay with this space between us. We grew accustomed to it, as all couples eventually do. We settled into our respective places in the relationship, happy that we could be the protector of the other's solitude.

I knew that if there was ever something of real consequence that I couldn't bring myself to share with her, that then our togetherness would be truly compromised.

Maybe I can never redeem myself. Maybe trying to explain any of it is just another narcissistic endeavor in a line of thinly masked efforts at self-preservation. I'm just an asshole. That's how Chloe will always see it. Probably how Cyb sees me, too.

The only thing I can say is that I was just doing what I thought could give her the best shot at a second happiness.

Maybe that changes nothing. At the least, I hope that it shows that I had good intentions.

Maybe it should be known that I suffered without her,

too. That I drove by her house at all hours of the day. That I, nearly, sent one thousand pitiful heartsick text messages. That I cried on the floor of the bathroom, our bathroom. That I yearned for Tito to keep me up at night, crying at the bed post to be let out. The wanting never stopped.

But I did my best to keep my yearning for her from her. I didn't want to make it any worse than it already was.

Even now, I hold back. After all I've put her through, it would not be fair. Not at all.

Maybe happiness came too early for us, she emailed the evening after she came over to my house, when I told her that I had gotten better, that I would likely be fine. We had it too good in our pretty-bodied years. So when C. broke down the door we had not prepared. We had taken no precautionary measures, established no security systems, failed to lock our precious belongings up in a safe. All of it, all of the happiness was right there on the kitchen counter for C. to take. We were naive. Too happy too early.

When I learned about M., I realized I was naive to think that she never kept things from me. Still, I'm kept up by this anxiety, wondering what I never knew about her, what I won't ever know. It's funny.

Beau

When we found out Pat would live, for a time, things got worse. Chloe and I were snacking at a rest stop sixty miles from my apartment. We got farther than we thought, driving and driving with Faron Young and Loretta Lynn.

She said, "I wasn't expecting the color in his cheeks when he opened our—I mean, his—front door. I wasn't expecting his biceps."

"You were not expecting that," I said, feeding her a piece of cheese on cracker. It had poured rain a few hours earlier. Despite the sun that followed the downpour, the dampness still pressed through our blanket, making everything just a little bit uncomfortable.

She said, "He led me to the couch, which I didn't recognize. There was a coffee table, too—hideous. One of those iron-and-glass-top things that only a man without a woman could find appealing."

"What were you drinking?" I asked.

"French press. Did you know, in the winter, we had to roll up towels and shove them up underneath the doorframe? The house could get so drafty."

I wiped my hands on the cloth napkin and dabbed crumbs from the edge of her lip.

"He was not completely put back together, you know." She rubbed her fingers along the frame of her lips. "People say someone who's ill is all *skin and bones* but I think the thing you notice really is the skin. Like the color of him's changed from fawn to porcelain."

"How did that make you feel?" I fed her again. She wiped her lips again.

"Good."

A siren wailed on the highway. An ambulance sped by us, close, but kept going on away from us.

"What did you discuss?"

"He asked if I wanted to see the CT scan. I said yes."

I did not say, *Why would you do that to yourself?*

"I told him it was beautiful."

I did not say, *Oh, Chloe.*

"I asked if I could keep it."

And of course, he let her keep it. It's hanging on her wall now, over her toilet, framed in an ornate gold antique that was falling apart but that we glued back together in her kitchen, together.

She said she cried in his arms and he carried her up to bed.

Later she said that was a lie.

But truthfully, she said he said, *I'm not forgetting you.*
She said, I forgot my coat there, too.

After that, Chloe and I were bathing together at least twice a week.

A month or so after she went to his house, we saw a woman being zipped up into a bag in the grocery store parking lot. The paramedics had set her bag of groceries on top of the gurney, as if she still needed them. She looked middle-aged, like she had had half a life. On the drive back to Chloe's, we wept.

We were nothing like Bonnie and Clyde. We played Cruelty, we had it in us, but we did not want it to be us. We wanted—

Family Room

When a child draws a picture of a house, Bachelard says, it signifies something about his childhood. If he draws a geometric structure with a neat roof and tidy yard, then he is representing the happiness of his rearing. If he draws a crooked house with two walls and no roof or windows or not even a doorknob, he is communicating the dilapidation of his homelife. "When the house is happy, soft smoke rises in gay rings above the roof."

I have no child to draw pictures of this house but let's just say he existed. I want to create a home that would bring light to this child. I want him to be able to draw a tidy square house with symmetrical lengths and widths and boxes of petunias set below two square windows and a rectangular door with a large yellow doorknob. I want him to draw two trees with orbular red fruits adorning its chestnut branches. I want him to break apart the house and show its hearth, which is forever glowing with a red-blue fire. This is his family room. This is his happiness.

Among a crowd of homeless men living in Waterloo Station, Gavin Bryars recorded one particular man who happened to be singing.

Bryars returned to his recording studio and copied the loop onto a continuous reel of tape. Then he went to have an espresso. When he came back, a group of people, techs and engineers and studio haunts, were sitting in the room, some quietly weeping.

"What happened?" he asked, worried some global catastrophe, another school shooting in America or a police officer murdering a black child, had taken place while he burned his lip on cheap Cuban espresso from a tin.

Listen, they said.

Looping on the record player, twenty-six minutes of a man's devotion.

I open my computer, find a link to the recording, and send it to Pat. I imagine him playing it as he falls asleep, waking in the night to the loop still rolling, *Jesus's blood never failed me yet* echoing out into the hallway. I imagine him stepping onto the cold bathroom tile, the hairs on his legs stiffening as he takes a piss, the sound of the piss hitting porcelain ringing in the quiet of our house, his house alone now, causing him to realize how alone he really is, the cancer (The Great Puts-It-All-Into-Perspective Device) no longer there to mask his solitude, a big, black blanket that smothered all other senses, the emotional ones, too. Now, the piss is an alarm.

* * *

All the candles are lit in the house. All the white ones I ordered online at a bulk price. I have not hung any decorations otherwise, but the candles do the trick. It is Christmas Eve and our little family is in the kitchen, assembling dinner, Tito and Beau and Mom and me.

"A motley crew, aren't we?" Mom says, placing the goose on the wood table, yet to be dented.

"Nowhere I'd rather be," Beau says, filling the wineglasses red to the rim.

"What are we missing?" I stand by the oven with my hands mittened, arms akimbo, apron floured.

"Nothing, sweetie," Beau says.

"Nothing, sweetie," Mom says. "Sit."

There is too much food but we all love to eat, in our own way. Mom will only eat a bite of this, a bite of that. Beau will fill his plate to the rim, layering goose with gravy with mashed potatoes with cranberry sauce. I will go back for seconds. Tito will lick our white plates.

"Take that off and sit down," Beau says, lifting the apron off my neck.

The three of us around a round table. When we cheers we rouge our lips, we dot the new white tablecloth, creating a kind of memento of the occasion, a work of art, some kind of Kusama.

They are okay, these stains. Lived in, this house becomes home.

The things that never had a chance to come into our home:

- Television set (Pat and I both had no use for it, a distraction, an ugly box, the great technological threat to feng shui.)

- Linen bedsheets, on the list, "One Day"
- Bookshelves that functioned as doors to another room, where we could disappear from dinner guests, my kisses rubbing along his ear while glasses clinked in the living room
- Baby monitor

Like many precious rituals of the past, kura skymning (or halla skymning) is fading from Scandinavian life. According to this particular tradition, at dusk, the individual must sit in silence, jettisoning all distractions, and let his brain wander off in any direction it needs. He must not fidget with his cell phone or bicker about who forgot what on the grocery list. His duty is meditation.

Once dark arrives, he turns on the kitchen light and returns to the lentils.

In the family room, I sit facing a wall, which someone intended to host a television (the ugly cords dangling like entrails), and look at it. I do not close my eyes. I am here. I keep dusk for myself.

Front Door

Good morning, Reno. Good morning, Chloe.

Hello, Roger.

Do you see this sunrise?

I saw it. It's passed now. But it was beautiful, yes.

It's just coming up here in the desert and it's something else.

Where are you going?

It's a quiet morning, which makes me worry. Something is going on that we aren't picking up on. Criminals are smart this morning.

And dumb other mornings?

Less careful. Are you okay? You've been listening to me a lot?

There was something about the way you say certain words.

Like?

Like "Good morning, Reno."

What about it?

There's something about you, unlike the others.

I guess you're not one hundred percent incorrect about that.

Thank you for talking.

It's my pleasure. Will you still be listening?

At least for a little while. You're good company.

Is it strange, ma'am, to say it's comforting to me to know you're out there?

Not at all, which probably says something about me, doesn't it?

Nothing that isn't good, I don't think.

That's a generous opinion.

You can count on me, Chloe.

Have a good day out there, Roger. Be safe, please.

I'll do my best, ma'am.

Around the anniversary of the sixth month in the new house, I thought about not doing this anymore. Why couldn't I escape, put the house on the market, rent an apartment in a sweaty town on the Gulf or a remote cabin in northern Maine, give up on this project of home making? After half a year, the house still felt like a hotel, devoid of character and warmth, a shell of a space meant for people's fantasies, romantic and twisted. I imagined myself alone in this house after another six months, lying on the guest room floor, swallowing sleeping pills in the bed-less, lamp-less, comfort-less room.

But I'm not that person. I couldn't possibly stain the recently refinished hardwood floors. People don't like to move into houses where murders and suicides have happened. Yes, the potential buyers would get a good deal on this renovated, updated home, but, still. I can never again be the person to spoil another's fantasy of home.

The house is nowhere near finished, whatever that means. It is likely that I'll be painting baseboards, installing light fixtures, caulking the windows of the shed, for years. I'm learning patience. That's just as much part of the process as trips to Home Depot, appointments with the handyman.

I'm not going anywhere.

New Addition

Let's say this child existed, or could exist.

How would he exist? Beau says, sitting on the edge of the bath, I in my towel on the lid of the toilet.

Would we—

No, he goes. We couldn't. He knows we must sit in proximity to one another's nakedness. *We could use a surrogate, if you were opposed to carrying—*

No—I wouldn't want that. I'd want the weight of him, of her.

I fold my arms across my chest. A cold, pre-snow gust blows in from the shower. I get up to close the window.

Your ass, it's getting big, I say.

I will be saying the same of you, soon enough.

I leave the bathroom, leaving him standing alone, return in jeans, a clean white T-shirt.

He takes my hands in his, like a movie man about to utter his proposal. *I am so happy to give this to you.*

On the floor, the little heater cooks. He stoops to turn the knob.

With a baby, you will have to be more sensible than to keep the heater on and the windows open. Whatever will the child learn?

I press my hand to his lips. *You can't do that. You won't be allowed to do that.*

I know. I will know when to shut up. You are the King and Queen.

Lullaby

Practicing lullabies?

Yes. Her text comes to me deliberately, with forward motion. So when he comes I won't be holding him in one arm and Googling song lyrics in the other.

Henri and I are on a walk in the neighborhood. He pulls at the leash. He chokes himself with yearning for the neighbor's collie we pass on the road. There is no sidewalk. We walk in the middle of the street. He is no good at this but we are trying something new.

Give me five and I will call you, I text back.

We are not far from the house and I was not planning any sort of set walk, so we go to the cul-de-sac at the end of the road and loop us back, toward my house.

"It is okay, Henri. It is okay."

His mouth waters endlessly on the leash, his body wanting something his brain cannot yet fully comprehend. Maybe this is what it has been like for Chloe. Her eyes scanned the facades of houses, her hands tucked cotton sheets under mattresses, all while her mind said, *Won't this be nice for a child?*

"Let's get you dried off, Henri."

Underneath this rag of a beach towel, his body moves in harmony with the gestures of my drying. I push and pull the towel against him, and he arches his back against my hands. There is so much to be said about the love of a dog, but now is not the time for that. Now is the time for Chloe, and—

Which song would you like to know?
Any, she texts. All.
This will be easier if I write them down. Email work?
Yes. Perfect.

I've situated my desk against a window that overlooks the pond. Depending on the season, I watch the geese circling and calling, the children in the paddleboats circling and calling. In April I sit here and prepare my taxes and in December I sit here and write Christmas cards. This desk has remained the same desk for thirty years. My routines I have kept with me as much as possible, a pattern against the chaos of the world.

And one day, I will be gone and there will be new patterns, new cycles, new stays against the world. That's what I've attempted to do for Chloe: to give her a cycle she could rely on. It may not have been the most exciting childhood, but didn't you feel loved? Didn't you never not feel whole of love?

Chloe,

This is one of the songs I sang to you over and over. You will have to try it out and see if it fits for you and the Baby. You will never know until you try it for yourself.

> *Hush little baby, don't say a word,*
> *Mama's gonna buy you a mockingbird,*
> *And if that mockingbird don't sing,*
> *Mama's gonna*

"Still soggy? I'll get back to you in a moment. Wait."

> *And if that diamond ring is brass,*
> *Mama's gonna*

"Got a case of the zoomies, Henri? Okay. Okay. One second."

> *And if that looking glass gets broke,*
> *Mama's gonna*

"Let's go, baby, let's get you toweled off for good."

Beau

An emu! That's what I thought when you came out of your mother. Not any emu, but one I saw walking down a feeder road off of I-10 as a boy. He was not supposed to be there, of course. He looked, as much as a bird can look, lost. He did not know where to go. From the backseat of my daddy's truck, I watched him walk along the fencing of a cattle ranch, a tall, lost bird. Finally, he, she, was out in the open world, unfettered.

Maybe it was the way you came out of your mother, a round little head and eyes that bulged out of your red face. You were, like your mother, unusual. You were all eyes and mouth, like you couldn't wait to see what followed the light, to shout your existence. Positivity is a good thing. It's not a trait your mother or I have—I'm not sure where you got that from, perhaps your mother's biological mother. But I know it's a rare quality in a person these days, one that will set you apart.

Of course you, like the emu, were headed into a complicated situation, into a complicated world, and you're a complicated boy. But you're ready for it. I believe that.

For the first time I'm hopeful. Good things are happen-
ing. I sound so damn cheerful. The twenty-two-year-old me
would think me a fool.

Happy birthday, Ru. The first of many, many, many. Kisses,
cher.

What superpower would you have? In the top left-hand corner
of my screen, his question arises at the bottom of a box, a
space Ty and I are carving out together.

Beau: You're starting with the serious questions.

Tyler: Well?

Beau: Well . . .

Tyler: I'm waiting.

Beau: Okay okay I'd have to say

Tyler: ?

Beau: To stretch time.

Tyler: How so? To make it faster or shorter?

Beau: Both. Longer and shorter than time as we experience it.

Tyler: What would the point of that be?

Beau: Well. We could hold on to moments we wanted to stay in and we could skip over the ones we didn't want to.

Tyler: I see. What moment would you hold on to?

Beau: You know what moment. How long have we been on here tonight?

Tyler: Let's not think about it that way.

Beau: I don't think about it that way. I'm just nervous. You make me nervous.

Tyler: That's ridiculous. Come on. We know each other.

Beau: I don't know. It's been so long. I have to go. Ru's crying.

Tyler: I can't believe you're a baby daddy. Actually, I can. Even as a kid, you were maternal. You held those puppies we found behind the Save More dumpster in such a way.

Beau: A baby daddy of sorts. More of a part-time baby daddy.

Tyler: Where is she?

Beau: Chloe? She's on a date.

Tyler: Good for her.

Beau: I think that she's finally ready again.

Tyler: I've missed you.

Beau: I haven't seen you in a millennium. You don't know me.

Tyler: We both know that's not entirely true.

Beau: There's time to figure this out. I'm not in a rush. You have no competition here in the country.

Tyler: You have no competition out here in L.A.

Beau: Hush.

Tyler: Goodnight, B.

Beau: Goodnight, Ty.

Before you were born, after your mother first moved into your house, I spent a lot of time worrying about her, though worrying was not a part of my upbringing. I wasn't raised to be such a heady person, always drowning in my own thoughts. Back in Dog Hill, men were supposed to *chercher à malfaire*, knuckles bared and whiskey imbibed. Boys were bred and beat to grow up blood and bone and gristle. If he turned out right, a man would have the world in a jug and a stopper in his hand. Driving in his truck, Daddy'd tap along to the radio on the steering wheel, slapping red time on my summer knees. *Ta maison est brûlée. Ta femme elle est pas là*, he'd chant, nearly shouting, soft Sunday drunk. *Elle a quitté hier au soir. Pour s'en revenir avec moi!* At that line, he'd take a swig of beer from the can in the console and pass it to me, little me, eight or ten or twelve years old. *Your house is burnt, and your wife is not there. She left last night, to be back with me.*

I did worry. Maybe that worrying helped your mom. In my own way, I did what I could to help her.

I think you were the real cure for her pain. For mine, too.

After all this time, Ty and I've found one another. Actually, he found me, on Facebook, where all lost people are found these days. We talk every day. Not on the phone, yet. Just over text. Over email. Over Facebook Messenger. We're not ready to break the three-decades-plus of silence. Once we hear the other's voice, there will be expectations. There will be real dreams. Right now, it's all harmless. Our longing is tempered by the intangibility of the web.

The phone rings and rings and rings on the kitchen counter. "Pick up the phone, Beau." Hours later, on a voice message, Ty's pleading echoes in the apartment. "Don't you want to be happy? Don't you want that? Jesus."

For my seventeenth birthday, my mother gave me a plastic Jesus, though I didn't have a car. She had wrapped him up in blue tissue and tucked him at the bottom of a shiny red-and-blue-striped bag. *When you leave this place, He will take care of you.*

I had not said I was leaving, but she knew my marks in school and that a quiet young man with a fondness for stray animals and books was never going to make a life in this corner of the South.

He will show you all the love you'll ever need, she said, a preacher not believing her own gospel.

"Do you want me to be the type of man to show up on your doorstep uninvited? Because I know you want me there, you just can't ask. Ask, Beau."

"I want you to show up on my doorstep."

"Really?"

"This is all just a ruse, isn't it? You must be married with a child and a bulletproof glass house. I'm just a flirtation."

"That's not it at all and you know it. It's just I never thought you'd actually say it."

"Of course I want you."

We could have made Ru a number of times, a million times, a time like this one:

"You make things up," Chloe said. All I could see of her was her right foot, a sliver of metatarsal and toes dangling over the edge of the tub.

I fanned the magazine's pages wide open at her. "That's the headline. See?"

"It doesn't say that at all," she said, grabbing the magazine with wet fingertips. "It's saying just the opposite. Why We Need Time Zones. And stop picking at your face."

"But," I said, turning from the mirror. I stopped picking.

"Just think if we abolished time zones. If we lived in Fiji, we could wake up on Tuesday and go to bed on Wednesday."

"I don't think it would affect either of us very much. Neither of us work normal jobs." Her foot receded back into the tub. Water whirled down the drain.

"If we lived in Fiji, we wouldn't be working the jobs we have now. I'd be a fisherman and you'd be a fisherwoman. We would wake up on Thursday and go to bed on Friday."

"You hate fishing."

"That's beside the point."

"Then what's the point?"

With her hand, she shooed me out of the bathroom. I closed the door behind me. Tito stayed with her. Water drip dripped off of her onto the tile. He licked, licking licking, the puddle forming around her feet.

"What's the point?"

"The point is," I said, the faucet rushing over my voice, "we would have a different life."

The door opened. Back then she wore her hair bobbed long, and she had combed it flat against her ovular head, hair slicked smooth with water so that the strands stuck to her nape. Around her, she wore an ugly terry cloth robe that I had given her. I'd read somewhere that it was the most comfortable piece of clothing imaginable, and she needed comfort.

"Isn't that always the truth?" she said. "How one altered detail can change everything?"

This robe was hideous, but it did what it was supposed to, hugged you in close, made you feel at home, wherever you were. I bought one for Chloe at the beginning of her home making.

"Your imagination needs a leash," she said. "The kind they put on toddlers."

"You know it's harmless."

"Of course I do. You're no evil genius." She rested her head against my chest. Her pillowed, tufted body quivered. The night was over. She took my chin in her fingers and said, "Stop picking."

"I can't," I said, picking at a whitehead on my forehead. "I've been practicing this craft since I was fifteen. I can't stop now."

"You have to leave now," she said, walking down the hall to her bedroom.

"You have a good night," I said.

But we did not. We never did. Ru could not have been made in a bed. We were not the kind of couple who could perform such an act of creation. Our family would be different, from conception forward.

"Where do you want the couch?" The moving man looks at my apartment, the sea of unstained white carpet. In the center of the room lies a three-by-five rug Chloe picked out for me at an antique mall before Ru was born. She had said, *Now that you've helped me, it's time for me to help you—and besides, Ru will need a place that feels like home when he's there.* When the doctor told us that the procedure had worked, that she was pregnant, I invited her over. It was time, after all this time of bantering, bathing, tending to her, creating a child together, for her to see where I slept. On first seeing my place, empty as a sailor's promise, she said, *Oh, Beau.* A week later she bought me the rug, all orange and blue diamonds, inviting color to the white space.

The rug is too small for the room. The two beautiful moving men look at me and think, *It is too small.*

"Evidently, anywhere," I say. "Where would you put it?"

"How about right here?" the other moving man says, gesturing with his chin to his partner. An inky purple honeysuckle grows out from the top of his T-shirt and blooms on his Adam's apple. They set the couch down in the middle of what most would consider a living room, facing a window that looks out over my small street.

"Seems right to me," I say.

"How long have you been living like this?"

"I should be offended, but you are not completely out of line in asking. Five years."

They wipe their foreheads at the same time with matching blue bandanas.

"Well," the one with the neck tattoo and white teeth says, "better late than never." I want to press my lips to the flower, suck the nectar.

The pretty movers leave the apartment. I lie down on the too-little rug, feeling all the space for the first time.

To a child, the drive out to the duck blind is timeless. In the dark in the warmth of Daddy's truck you feel as if you are in a womb, warm and full of potential, eager. Perhaps that's where this desire for you started. Maybe fatherhood in its own strange shape was something I was waiting for my whole life. Maybe I was conscious of you in some way, as a little boy in the back of my own father's truck. Maybe that anticipation was for something bigger than the hunt. Maybe it was for the day when I would have my own little boy to bounce around in my own truck. All I'm saying is that it makes sense that you are here.

"I wouldn't say this about your art, but as far as home making, *Those who can't do, teach* really does apply here."

"It's a matter of desire, dear. If I had wanted to make this place look nice, I would have."

Chloe gives me a look before her drill screws the curtain rod bracket into the wall.

"These curtains will be perfect. Ty will think I am some sort of Lord Byron with all this velvet."

"That was my intention!"

"I can't hear you!"

"Your curtains are hung!" she screams, though I can hear her fine now. "Take me to lunch. I want a fish sandwich with big fat French fries."

"Only the fattest for you, love."

We are both a little bit too sweaty and a little bit too tired for dining out, but we leave the apartment and walk down the street toward the corner pub that is slightly Irish and slightly yokel and has the right carefree atmosphere for our current moods. She orders French fries fried in bacon fat and a glass of wine and I order a salad and tap water.

"He must really be special if you're skipping these."

"It's not for him," I clarify. "It's for me."

She gives me another look.

"Perhaps it's for the both of us. It doesn't hurt, you know, to be healthy once in a while."

"I hope I get to meet him, but if not, I understand."

"I would like you to. Ru, as well, if you wouldn't mind."

"I do not mind. You both should come over. I will cook something. Is he a vegan, vegetarian?"

"How did you know?"

She looks at my plate, at my face.

"Thank you for your help with the apartment. God-willing he will be impressed by me."

"He will swoon." She takes my face in her hands and kisses my forehead. She holds up a French fry to my mouth and I take it. I fork a bite of greens and feed her. "Just a few more weeks," she says, and she is right.

I look at my phone's calendar, my imminent schedule cleansed of teaching and office hours and administrative meetings for the academic break, my mornings and afternoons to be reserved for studio time, my evenings for quiet, for thinking, Saturday afternoons for Ru, and then, Ty will be here, and for one week, we will have all the time in the world.

Drip. Drip. Drip. From the ceiling and onto the kitchen island. It is cold outside and the rain is coming hard though it shouldn't be coming at all like this in January but we are not worried.

"Of course, when you finish the bathroom, something else falls apart," I tell Chloe, bourbon in our hands, the light hovering over us. Ty arrives in two days.

"It's fine. I've come to expect it as a constant project."

Her cheeks are rosy, not from blush, fever, or flu. Just health and happiness.

"I'm baking his cake tomorrow and you will get the balloons and—" She pauses, licking the alcohol on her finger from a clumsy sip. "What else are we missing?"

"We have everything. His birthday party will be a bash, a blowout, the party of the year."

She takes another, cleaner sip and knits the liquor into her lips. "The best party of the year in this house, anyway."

She is seeing someone now, someone who I can actually tolerate. He brings Ru books he cannot yet read. He takes Chloe and Tito to the dog park, though Tito is more of a hobbler now than a runner and just sits in their laps the entire time, just so he can be around his kind. He will not come to the party because he is a good man and understands it is too early for him.

Ru is crying through the baby monitor and Chloe has set down her glass to go to him.

"I'll go and get him," I say. "You enjoy that Booker's. If you don't, I'll be offended."

The nursery doesn't look like a nursery at all. It has no cutesy anything anywhere, no mural with giraffes and elephants, no oversized stuffed animals. The overall impression is a sea of blue on which a white bassinet gently rocks. Without words, I pull him to my chest. He stops crying. He has my glacial forehead and Chloe's expressive lips and time will tell what of either of our personalities he has, though I sense that he has our curiosities as well as our sensitivities, which will make him vulnerable but empathetic. He could be stubborn like me, like Chloe, or maybe he will be like Cybil, not stubborn at all, open to the world's fluxes, its cruelties. Maybe he will be a good baker, like my mother, or perhaps he will flounder in the kitchen but will always remain persistent, always trying, like his mother. Maybe he will cuss like my father, drink like my Cajun blood portends. We cannot wait to see what he will be, but we can also wait, don't want to rush him into his future. Ru and I wait in an easy silence. There will be plenty of time for words tomorrow.

Tyler: I'm about to get on the plane.

Beau: I'll be there to pick you up at 5:14, three minutes to spare, enough time to ensure my lipstick pops just right 😉

Tyler: Haha. Do you remember right before you moved to Texas how I drove us up to Natchitoches and my aunt made us go on that holiday house tour with her?

Beau: Vaguely. My mind wasn't quite there then, as you likely remember.

Tyler: Really? You nearly punched the homeowner when he told us the slave quarters were *exquisite.* You always were a little warrior.

Beau: I do remember that.

Tyler: My aunt also tried to set you up with my cousin Amber. You weren't having it.

Beau: I was feverish with pain. You missed me bursting by a few months. Glad you were spared.

Tyler: I never knew how badly you suffered. You never showed it.

Beau: Texting is not the best place for this . . . but the short of it: My sister had died a month before we went up to Natchitoches. And I was going to lose you, too.

Tyler: You had gone through a lot.

Beau: I won't let you out of my bed all week.

Tyler: I'm happy. Are you happy?

Beau: Happier than ever.

Tyler: Safe travels on that long road to the airport.

Beau: You too 🙏, in your own way.

Daddy's dead now. Mama, she moved back to Lake Charles after twenty-five years in Texas, happy as a lifetime smoker with a dead daughter and a penchant for Catholic asceticism can be. We talk now and then, though she doesn't know much about me, and that's really for the best. Weather and promotions and am I eating good (of course, Mama, the holy trinity is alive and well in me). My brothers and sister don't know much either, though they know some things, and that's why they don't say much anymore.

I have blood and bone, the same blood and bone as them, but sometimes that's not enough.

We want you to have a home. We want you to feel like you have a place to return to. Even if this home is not easy to categorize, it has its own shape, its own weight. Even if the yard's a little overgrown and the house's painted purple in a neighborhood of eggshell houses, it's a place to come back to.

"You needed to get out of L.A. How is this? Is this different enough?"

There is not much to do where I live, much like where I grew up, so I am driving Ty around the country. A colleague of mine owns this land, around two thousand acres. Not farmland. Just land. Lots of it. His son tends to it. He plants fruit trees. He plants sunflowers and corn for the deer and rabbits and bears. My colleague says he never eats any of it, which I've found to be a generous but strange behavior, one of those idiosyncrasies that makes people truly interesting. In the winter field, corn lies in dried husks.

"I didn't necessarily *need* to get out of L.A.," he says. "I came here to see you."

"Do you want to go up in the blind? It's the nicest duck blind you ever did see."

"You still hunt?" He hands me the thermos full of wine. The road through Randall's land is unpaved and we jostle up and down and around in my truck. I wait to drink until I stop at the base of the blind.

"From time to time." Sometimes I tell Randall that I'm going hunting, but all I do is sit up there with a thermos full of coffee and Baileys. He thinks I'm a bad shot because maybe once a season I come back with a deer or turkey but I don't mind him thinking so. Sitting up there is the most peaceful thing in the world.

Ty's life has changed. Ty moved on to cities, New York, Portland, L.A. Mine, however, has stayed quiet. I prefer the same country stillness, the small-town life. So much of my life has changed that I prefer the same old cattle and quiet.

"Get your gloves on," he tells me, setting mine in my lap. He is buttoning up and pulling a beanie down over his ears. Getting out of the truck, he puts the two thermoses into his backpack and slides the straps over his shoulders. Hands on his lovely hips, he says, "Ready?"

You first, I do not say, trying to avoid easy joking, *in case you fall and I need to give you mouth-to-mouth resuscitation.*

"No ladder? Fancy setup he's got here."

Randall has built a set of stairs up to the blind. He is an older gentleman. He likes his hunting refined.

I watch his ass move up the ladder. I could make a joke, compliment him again, but I don't. I stay quiet.

Up in the blind, I pat the space next to me on the wooden bench, which has been cushioned with two pads adorned with flowers, the kind you'd see on Mawmaw's kitchen chairs. He doesn't speak either. We sit, watching the field. In a few months, birds will hatch and some will fall out of their nests, and soon mother birds will mourn and hatch more eggs. Soon, a black bear will crawl out of her cave and kill a rabbit, the juice on her jowls an elixir bringing her out of winter. Now, I want to tell Ty I love him, that I want to fuck him in this blind where no one can hear us, that I want to lick the wine from his lips and afterward open my truck door for him, kiss him on the cold cheek that was just pressed up against the cold air, to tuck him into my bed and cook him dinner, to move him here and ask for his hand, to care for him, to tend to him for the rest of our lives, to tend to one another in the way that we never could, to make red beans in the kitchen and talk about how we'd never have boudin as good as what his daddy would make in Lake Charles, to, in the spring, get married in a field just like this one, maybe even this one, where he can walk across the field with a bouquet of sunflowers in his hands, and I can touch those hands, take them in my own, kiss them, kiss them, hands as dear to me as my own.

"It will snow tomorrow," I say.

"Maybe my flight will get delayed. Maybe I'll be stuck here." He kisses me, his tongue finding all of me. I am weak.

"It is too cold. I can't send you back there with a cold. Let's go and I'll make you dinner."

We pack up, go down the stairs, and get back in the truck. Driving, we pass a small graveyard set under an undisturbed gathering of oaks.

"Can we get out and see?" he asks.

I stop the car, leaving the engine running. We get out and walk around to the humble entrance. The wrought-iron fence has collapsed in places, tilting in where it was supposed to keep out. Little tombstones, many of the etchings washed away by years of rain and snow and wind, poke out of the earth. A few larger stones lay flat, the ground beneath them no longer positioned to carry their weight. We read still-visible names and dates. Father. 1822 to 1876, or something close to it. Mother. 1826–1888. There are no houses on this land anymore, but I tell him there once was one nearby, up on a hill not far from here. This is where this family lived and died, on this land where sunflowers now stand, their seeds eaten by deer and squirrels and rabbits, a place where humans only visit from time to time. Here, people are no longer troubled by the possibility of building houses. This land is no longer for them. They are free.

"It's getting late," I tell him, pinching his cheek between my gloves. "You're not properly dressed."

"It's not so sad, is it," he says, and I do not think he expects an answer.

We drive through the field, up and down in the dark, back toward the lights of town.

Nursery

You can always come home, I tell Ru. We are sitting on Ru's bed in the room that Beau and I had once painted blue like the sea, the room in which we had assembled a white crib over white wine and potato chips, the room that became a nursery that became a big boy's bedroom. Ru's toys and books are in boxes piled against the wall. The date for the move has been set. In a few weeks, I tell him, we will be moving to a new place, a place that is also home.

"It all started right here." I place my hand on my stomach. "You waited and waited in this warm bath, giving a kick every now and then to show me you were waiting for me, waiting to get out into the world. I've never told you this story before, have I?"

Ru shakes his head. He is six years old now. I want him to understand why we're moving South, to a place where heat envelops you, comforts you.

"You came out screaming—eight pounds, six ounces. You were a chunky little thing with a big head. You were so healthy. We weren't at the hospital long."

Ru is old enough to learn where he came from, where he is going. I explain who this man is who he calls *Uncle*—he is not really that, a blood and bone uncle, anyway. I explain that this man, Uncle Beau, is my best friend, my confidant, *his* confidant, his godfather. I explain that though he is not on the birth certificate as *Father*, Ru shares half of his DNA, making him part creator, making him a certain type of family that he's known in his gut since he came out screaming.

"So Uncle Beau will live here when we go?" Ru asks. He is fixated on the leaving, on the old house, on the past, and he is right, the past is part of this.

"Beau will move out of the apartment and live here, yes. While I complete my graduate work, that is how it will be."

"He will not get rid of my bed?"

"He will not get rid of your bed."

This has been a good house to us. This is where we picked worms out of the garden dirt and placed them in a terrarium by his bedside, the same room where I found him in the dark talking to the worms, assuring them the night would not be a dangerous one, that morning would surely come. This is where we spent July and August afternoons in the plastic pool inflated in the yard, where we read storybooks together in his little bed until we both fell asleep, this little bed where we watched movies on a little screen I held between us, the same screen on which I'm now showing him the street that he will one-soon-day run down. Though we will soon leave this house, I want to ensure Ru that the sandy-desert paint color of the bathroom, the smoky haze of the living room after I'd burn the piñon incense in the fall, the fainting couch in the window where he'd fall asleep, in my arms, at first, and then on his own, those things will always be here for him.

"Beau will be here, whenever you want to see him. Whenever you want to see the house, you can visit."

He ducks his head beneath the covers and I wrestle him out, bring him up for air.

"But there are other things out there to explore," I tell him.

"Why New Or-lee-ans?" he asks, pronouncing the name of the city like the radio announcer on WWOZ, who we've been listening to on the radio while we cook.

"I'm going to school, like you." I explain to him that no, I won't be a doctor like Grandma, but another kind of doctor, the kind who cures illnesses of places, who studies neighborhoods without grocery stores, cities without recycling bins. All those books on the shelves? There will be even more books in our new home in Louisiana.

We are going to New Orleans for reasons I can't fully explain. Because I got into a graduate program there and because it is free. Because I want to show Ru one aspect of his history. Because I want to give him context for the boy he is, for the man he will be. Because I want Ru to grow up in a place where being mixed, being a mutt, is something to celebrate. These are verbalizations, rationalizations, but maybe this move is about something you can't just put into words. Call it a mother's instinct. This place is right for Ru, for me, for us.

"Because Beau is from Louisiana, you are from Louisiana, too." I point to the alligator mouthing a saxophone on his T-shirt, brush his hair with the palm of my hand, kiss the head that is still too big for his little body, the head that may always be a little too big for his body. This is the T-shirt Beau gave him when I first told Ru we would be moving to New Orleans. That day, Beau put on a record, and out of the living room speakers came trumpet music, brass music, *feeling music*, as Ru called it. That was the day I first asked Ru to sit down next to me and look at photos of our new home, purple and yellow houses draped with bougainvillea, corner stores with hand-painted signs, men masked in beads and feathers strutting down a street that looked nothing like the street he lived on, a new world with a little white castle on the edge of a bayou.

Soon, we will hold on to those kisses from Beau and Grandma and drive down, all the way South until land meets water.

"Grandma will come to visit. Beau, too," I say. "This is not goodbye forever. Just goodbye for today."

When I told my mother about the move, she said, *You'll have a room for me.* We are leaving this house, Beau, Mom, but we are leaving so we can grow. Today, we are looking forward, not backward. This is not goodbye forever. Just goodbye for today.

New Builds

Home making in the Deep South. Home making for a child who is not yet home in his body. It's been barely a month in this new place when Ru says, *I want to see the music, I want to see the people*, so Chloe takes him out into the neighborhood on Lundi Gras, noonday, where costumed, boozed, happy people are standing around, unicorns and mermaids and mermen and robots and scarecrows and indescribable transformations that require no label; they are just fabulous. *Fabulous*, his mother whispers into his ear, pointing at someone like no one he has seen before up in that Southern North, in his first home. He has never been around such crowds, around so many people smiling and drinking and standing around in the street—his life has been so quiet, so remote from the noise of people. But this one person is the person he's fixating on, a boy who is maybe eighteen, nineteen years old, a shadow of stubble masked across the bottom half of his face, and Ru recognizes himself in this man, who is not like any him he's ever seen in Virginia, in his old home. And this boy has a beauty, has a *something* that rings true to him, something evident in his eyelashes dotted with rhinestones, the sequin-adorned triangles offering his chest modesty, the weave of black netting that stretches from ankle to hip. Ru pulls his long hair off of his face and ties it back with elastic, like his mom showed him, so he doesn't miss this person, so he doesn't lose him in the crowd. The crowd gets louder, begins cheering. They are ready for the parade. And this young man is standing on the corner, a drink in his hand, and he puts his arm around a woman, dressed like he is, exactly like he is, with the same rhinestone-lined eyes and sequin triangles, and he kisses her on the lips, right in the middle of the crowd.

This is to say that Ru's idea of the world splinters, like a spinning mirrored globe fractures light. Something in his chest releases, letting out built-up pressure. Relief he didn't even know he needed.

After that day, things are different for this family, again. Mom takes him home, and before you know it it's his eleventh birthday. His chest is hardening, his thighs filling out, what to do with these thighs, this chest, he thinks, looking in the mirror at what God has given him and draping it in scarves, tying his hair back into a knot at the nape of his neck, and he walks out into the house's small yard where his mother is typing, where she is working out on the patio, the banana trees backgrounding her sunlit frame, and the boy says, *What am I*, a statement, not a question, as if that is the answer, the question becoming a statement of identity. *No,* she corrects, *What I am,* and she beckons him to the arm of the aquamarine Adirondack, detangling the knots with humidity-soft fingers, twisting and twisting and folding the hair into a tight formation atop his head. Turning him around, she kisses him on the nose, takes out her phone, brings up the camera, and hands him the mirror to see what it now reflects.

Mother and son hands reach into Zapps, crunchy Crawtator crumbles all over their fingertips. Ru strikes a pose, flashing red-seasoned peace fingers, and Mom takes a photo, captioned, "Your boy's initiated," and sends it to Uncle Beau, who returns a ♡, a 🍠, 🍌), a 🍢. Ru sends his uncle, his father, his Family, a photo of Mom and himself, his head in profile, his new do framed by banana leaves, and Beau returns, simply, exactly, just what Ru needs, 😇.

Ruel, American Wakashu.

And he goes to school like this, in his uniform, khaki pants and a polo, with the same mage that his samurai fathers once wore to keep their helmets in place. *Do you do your hair like that*, the girls say. *Can you do my hair like that*, and he obliges them this at recess, especially one girl, Miranda, in whose hair he weaves a special, secret braid, and one of the boys says, *You look just like my mama, are you trying to be like her?* And he does not have an answer. He does not have a word for what he is.

In this new city, the parades march on, year by year. The brass bands play the same songs, with some variations, some new additions to the repertoire, but always *Oh, When the Saints* and *Mardi Gras Mambo Mambo Mambo*. Across the years, most of the dogs are named *Saint* or *Roux*, and all the children grow up knowing the difference between a sousaphone and a tuba. All the little boys and girls know how to twist off the tails and suck the heads, the crawfish meat worth the dirtying of fingernails, the stinging of cuts. All the boys and girls grow up knowing to avoid the potholes on their bikes, how to shake their asses. They know the symphony of gunshots as well as they know the radio Top 40. This is where Ru grows up, a place that shares his blood, the swamp juices composed of the same juices in his gut. This is home.

In this home, he sucks the heads, he shakes his ass, too.

This is home, isn't it? his mother asks him, she is always in the banana leaves, or, at least, that's how he will remember her, banana leaves forming a nimbus around her head. He is eighteen now, and he will nod, kiss his mother on the top of her head, with the height and humor of Beau, and he will go out on the Fourth of July with glittered eyelids and red-painted hair. On a bedroom floor Miranda will break open a pen, dip a needle into its ink, and poke her name into the skin of his thigh. *Don't forget, motherfucker!* And they give up their bodies to the other on the floor, seeing one another through two sets of glittered eyelids.

What am I, what I am.

Outside the house, bottle rockets flare down the street. Farther away over the river, bigger fireworks burn up on the city barge. Big booms, smaller pops. Beneath the flag flying over Miranda's mother's house, red white and blue, the red like his hair, they run toward the Mississippi. The pores of their skin flare open in the hot, wet night.

Yes, I am home, he will remember feeling. Finally, for now.

About the Author

Lee Matalone lives in South Carolina. *Home Making* is her first novel.